The Other Side of the Fence

By the Same Author

YOUNG RAZZLE   1949

SON OF THE VALLEY   1949

HIGHPOCKETS   1948

THE KID COMES BACK   1946

Published by Harcourt, Brace & Co.

A CITY FOR LINCOLN   1945

ROOKIE OF THE YEAR   1944

YEA! WILDCATS!   1944

KEYSTONE KIDS   1943

ALL-AMERICAN   1942

WORLD SERIES   1941

CHAMPION'S CHOICE   1940

THE KID FROM TOMKINSVILLE   1940

THE DUKE DECIDES   1939

IRON DUKE   1938

The Other Side of the Fence

of the Fence

by JOHN R. TUNIS

jT8340

New York   *1953*

William Morrow & Company, Inc.

The Other Side of the Fence

Chapter 1

HE poked his head around the corner of the living room. His mother was sitting in the big chair reading *Life,* or at least turning the pages and looking at the pictures.

"Mother."

"Yes, Robin."

"Can I . . ."

"No, you cannot have the station wagon this afternoon. I need it because I'm going to the Red Cross. It's Thursday."

"Oh." He vanished.

"Robin! Robin!" she called, as the screen door banged behind him.

"Yes, Mother." The door banged again and he entered the room, a tallish boy in blue shorts and a white skivvy shirt. His yellow hair contrasted with his tanned face.

"Robin, have you done your practicing today?"

"I was just going to."

"You better go do it right away. Please don't put it off until the afternoon. You know the first thing your father will ask when he steps off the five-thirty-one—'Has he been practicing or was he on the golf course all afternoon, wasting time?' "

"Uh-huh. I was just getting set. Mother . . ."

"Yes?" She turned another page of the magazine.

"Look, if I do my practicing, would you drop me off at three at the Fairfield Turnpike? Please?"

"All right. If you do your practicing, I will. But see here, Robin. Try to get back before your father comes. Do, please. He hates you to be late for dinner."

"O.K." The screen door banged again. He went out singing.

From the stone house perched on the point, the lawn sloped gently down to the sandy beach. There was a smell of salt in the air as he walked across the thick turf. Half a dozen small sailing craft were moving slowly toward the blue waters of Long Island Sound just beyond.

Robin glanced across the narrow harbor mouth at his feet to the town of Five Mile River and the opposite bank. He was so close he could hear the sound of the car horns over the water, and could see the men working in the red barns along the bank that had been turned into repair shops for small boats. It was a beautiful scene, a beautiful, warm June afternoon.

He walked slowly around the house to the side. Here the grass was as green, the turf as thick, as on the water front, except for a small brown path about one hundred feet long. This worn path led to an oblong space twelve or so feet square, filled with brownish sawdust. There was a high stick on each side of this pit, and a small bar balanced across the sticks. A wooden slab was sunk flush with the grass below the bar.

Slowly Robin went toward a pile of poles about fifteen feet long in the corner beside the kitchen window. He took one up, hefted it, inspected it carefully along its length, put it back, took another, looked it over, raised it to his shoulder as if it were a javelin. He walked toward the pit and laid the pole on the grass; then, placing his hands on his hips, he began kicking his legs vigorously into the air, first one and then the other.

From the kitchen window Fanny, the colored cook, glanced out and quickly turned away. She was entirely used to the scene. Every summer for years she had seen him go through the same process day after day. Now he was squatting, twisting his torso from side to side. Then he slipped over onto his stomach, and for a few minutes did push-ups. Rising, he trotted down the grass and turned back with a sudden burst of speed. At last he took the pole and, inserting it into the slot below the bar, he turned and twisted his body around it three or four times. Tossing the pole aside, he leaned over and walked around on his hands, his body still and erect.

He picked up the pole again and went to the end of the little worn path on the grass. There he stood motionless, the pole by his side pointed slightly upward. There was a frown on his face. Concentrating, he looked at the bar. Then he came up on his toes, alert, supple, and pranced slowly forward, gathering speed. His spikes bit into the grass. Faster he went, faster, so effectively you could tell he had done it a thousand times. The pole hit the ground, slipped into the little wooden slot; his body slowly rose in the air. It straightened out, the pole fell backward, and he was over the crossbar with inches to spare.

His mother watched from the kitchen window, thinking back to the times years ago when she had seen his father's figure rise, heave up against the sky, and fall gracefully to the dirt below. How many, many times she had held her breath as the bar wavered, joggled, and finally settled back into place. Or clattered to the ground while a sigh rose from the crowd. Robin was so like his father in his little gestures, the way he frowned as he stood on tiptoe, the pole like a lance at rest by his side.

Fanny stood beside her, watching too. "Looks like he's getting his practice in early today. I bet he's headed for that golf club this afternoon."

The station wagon moved slowly along the black-top road. It traversed leafy lanes, turning and twisting through the woods, with now and then a view of the Sound through the trees.

Robin's mother broke the silence. "Are you playing Butch Morrison again this afternoon?"

"Yes," he answered briefly.

"I don't like your seeing so much of him. He's not a good friend for you. His father is the town . . . the town . . ."

"The town what?"

"Why, you know. A good-for-nothing. Never held a job in his life."

"Know what, Mother? At the Democratic picnic last week at Roton Point he ate three dozen oysters and drank ten bottles of beer, all at one sitting, too, Mother."

She turned the wheel at a curve. "I wouldn't doubt it in the least. Robin, why don't you ever play with the Lonsdale boys or Michael Swann or those friends of yours over in Five Mile River?"

He laughed. "Because they're no good. Butch shoots a 39. That's when the course is empty, and Tommy Brogan lets him. Know something, Mother?"

"What?"

He hesitated before answering. Then suddenly it came out. "I don't wanta go to Yale."

"Robin, please don't say *wanta!* That's what comes of associating with Butch Morrison."

"Oh . . . all right. I don't . . . want . . . to go to Yale."

He realized instantly that she was upset by the way she clutched the wheel of the Buick. So he went on quickly, to get it all out and over with at once. "Almost . . . sometimes . . . I'd just as soon go to Princeton."

Now she was shocked. "Oh, Robin, please don't say these things when your father comes home. It's been so hot in New York today, and that contract was to be decided this afternoon. He'll be exhausted."

"O.K. But you know what, Mother? I've had Yale and pole vaulting ever since I was a kid. I've had 'em up to here." He drew his finger expressively across his throat, and his face looked as if he would like to cut it.

She laid her right hand on his knee affectionately. She understood how he felt, and she knew also that this had been a long time coming, that it had burst from him at an unexpected moment. Perhaps it meant something; possibly it was just a part of growing up, she was not sure. So she merely nodded.

He continued. "Mother, there were times when I was a kid and Dad used to take me up to the Bowl, I almost wished Harvard would win. I almost did, Mother."

She nodded and sighed. She understood his feelings perfectly. So she said nothing.

"There's a boy in my class at school, boy named John Poole. His father was an end at Cambridge, but he won't even go out for the team. Says he doesn't want to have to play in college; he hates football, just the way I hate pole vaulting. Once he told me he felt the same way I did about college, only about Harvard. He wants to go to the University of Chicago. The funny thing is, I always envied John Poole."

"That's all natural, I suppose. I wouldn't worry too much about it if I were you."

"No. But, Mother, I wish Dad had been a golf champ like Terry Foster's old man, instead of a pole vaulter. He made a hole in one last week on the fourteenth. Gosh, can he smack a golf ball! It screams. He drives an M.G. too, one of those low-slung, yellow-painted numbers."

She glanced at him. His tanned face was aglow. "If your father had been a golf champion, you would have been crazy about tennis. That's how life is, Robin. Well, here's the Turnpike. How are you going to get to the club from here?"

"Easy. I always nab a ride with the assistant pro. He goes home to dinner and passes right by here about this time."

She stopped the car. "All right. Just don't ride with any stranger."

"Nope, I won't, Mother." He waved at her and raced over to the edge of the Turnpike.

Late that afternoon Robin's father and mother were returning from the five-thirty-one. She was not driving and happened to see her son first. She clutched her husband's arm. "Why, there's Robin, up by the bridge. What on earth is he doing way over here?"

The car charged past, slowed down, and he rushed toward them, hot and disheveled.

"Robin!" his mother protested, as he climbed into the back. "Wasn't Pamela or anyone coming back from the club? I do wish you wouldn't hitchhike these days."

"Oh, Mother," he panted, "I'm . . . I'm old enough to handle myself. Old enough to have a driver's license, aren't I?"

"Certainly," Dad said firmly. "He's old enough to take care of himself now, Jane."

"I don't know what you two mean. He's had his driver's license exactly ten days, that's all." Yet she knew when both of them were against her that she would be defeated, so she said nothing more.

Chapter 2

THEY were all sitting on the stone porch, as they always did after dinner, watching the boats pass by. You got so you knew everyone's boat and just when they would take an evening sail on the Sound, when they would leave the harbor entrance and exactly when they would make it again later in the evening. What Robin and his mother were really waiting for was news of the contract, for they were a close family and always shared things. Robin's father, however, liked to be casual about big things, and he wanted to tell the story his own way in his own good time.

Finally he spoke. "Well," he said evenly, as if what he was saying was really of no great importance, "well, we got the white-wall-tire contract."

"No! Really! You didn't!"

"Yes. Twelve of the top agencies in New York were all in there pitching, but we grabbed it off. I must say I feel good about it."

"Well, you should," Robin's mother said with emphasis. "You ought to be pleased. You certainly worked long enough and hard enough on it, too."

"Oh . . . it was a team job. The boys all worked on it."

Robin listened with attention. He guessed that this evening might be the time to tackle his father about the trip, yet he didn't know exactly how to begin. After a while, when the excitement over the white-wall-tire contract had subsided a little and the deal had been explained so everyone understood it, he said timidly, "Know what, Dad? Know what I did today? Beat Butch three and two this afternoon."

A large white vessel with two decks glided out of the harbor below them. Robin's father never saw it; he was looking at the tanned blond boy in the blue shorts and the white shirt.

"Did you? Good lad, good boy, Robin. You must have been really hitting them."

"Yessir, I was shooting all right. Had a three on the fourteenth and a four on the ninth."

His father settled back and lit a cigarette. "Let's see now. You played golf today; you beat Butch Morrison for the first time . . . that correct?"

The boy nodded.

"And you never thought about practicing. You were out at the club all day long."

"No, *sir*. I practiced. Ask Mother if I didn't. I practiced over an hour. I was up around eleven-ten two or three times."

"Fine! That's not too bad, not too good, either.

But when I think how I felt when I did twelve feet as a sophomore in college . . ."

"The Olympic record is fifteen feet now, Dad."

"Yes, I'm quite aware of it. The world moves. Don't rub it in."

Inside, the telephone rang. "It's probably for you, Robin," said his mother. "It's Pamela Griswold, I should imagine, calling you." But Robin didn't jump; he didn't leap for the telephone as he usually did. So she rose and went into the living room.

"Dad, can I talk to you?"

"Proceed." His father was sitting with his hands in his pockets, the cigarette in his mouth, and that look on his face which showed he was on Madison Avenue and not at the moment in Five Mile River.

"No, seriously. I want to talk to you. Alone, I mean."

Robin's father took the cigarette from his lips and looked up quickly. "Robin, your mother is on the telephone with Mrs. Rodgers. If form holds, she'll be there at least twenty minutes. You have all the time in the world. What seems to be the trouble?"

"Well . . . h'm . . . Dad . . . I'm getting pretty stale. Honest I am."

"I shouldn't be in the least surprised. One does. But you must stay with it, son; that's the only way in the world you'll ever get there. Some day I expect to watch you clear that bar at fifteen feet."

"Oh, no. Not me. Never. Dad, didn't you ever get tired of practicing the pole?"

"Why, of course. Everyone gets tired of it. But there's no easy way; in fact, there's no other way except to keep at it."

Robin looked out across the water. A blue-sailed yawl was moving smoothly out through the narrow entrance below with a girl and a boy in the stern. It was Jackie Roberts with Phyllis Wallace. They waved up to him and he waved back.

Suddenly it all came out, everything he had been feeling for months, years perhaps: the dislike of the drudgery of practice every day, the whole dismal business of growing up to be just like your old man; having your entire life arranged for you, set, fixed. "And, look, Dad, I don't want to go to Yale!" He had not intended to say it, but it came out before he could stop himself.

Nothing happened. No earthquake; no tornado. The heavens didn't open, the house didn't tumble down, even the porch remained steady. The blue-sailed yawl still glided peacefully toward the open Sound.

Robin's father rose, stood with his back to the water, feet apart, hands in his pockets. The cigarette was turned upward, and his head tilted back to keep the smoke from his eyes. For a minute he said nothing. When he spoke, the voice was quiet and the tone was more contemptuous than angry. "Nonsense! Of course you want to go to Yale. You're a third-generation pole vaulter, aren't you? I want you to go there, and I believe you'll be a much better jumper some day than I ever was. Honestly, Robin, I doubt if you ever really amount to anything in golf. Just because you beat Butch Morrison, you know, doesn't say anything."

He was taking the blow pretty well, almost too well. But if he doesn't get annoyed, thought the boy, perhaps it would be a good time to go ahead and spring the trip on him. Only I do wish he'd be more serious about everything. He still believes I don't mean what I say. "No . . . no fooling! I'm . . . well . . . I can't exactly explain it . . . just that I'm tired of Yale and pole vaulting . . . and everything. I want . . ."

"What *do* you want, Robin?"

"I want to get away."

"Get away? Where to?"

"Butch Morrison is leaving in his car next week. He's going to work his way across the country and back. He wants me to go with him, Dad."

"Butch Morrison? Why, that's ridiculous. You two youngsters!" His father exploded. "At your age! You aren't even a freshman in college. It's absurd!"

"Look, Dad, remember how you always told me you ran away from home that summer and joined the merchant marine? Remember, you told me how you sailed to South America the summer before you went to Yale?" He was pleading now, trying to get his father to see another point of view. Usually Dad was so reasonable about things; he wasn't like most fathers. Mother was sometimes unreasonable, Dad never. Because he was a father and a lot more: he was a coach, who knew top-class pole vaulting as a champion; he was a friend who showed you how to handle a boat and what was wrong with your golf swing; he was an elder brother and you always felt close to him.

"Remember, Dad, remember?" he argued. Try and see things from my angle, his tone begged.

But his father shook him off. "Oh, I was older than you. I was eighteen . . . almost." He was rocked by the boy's determination. The cigarette in his lips was lifeless now. He turned and looked across the water to the lights starting to twinkle in Five Mile River. The beauty of the place struck him keenly. Why on earth should anyone want to leave such a lovely spot?

He sighed. I always imagined Robin loved the place, he thought. I always imagined he enjoyed being a pole vaulter and captain of the track team at school. I figured I was being the best father in the world. I took him sailing and played golf with him and talked about Yale and went to games in the Bowl . . . now he doesn't want to go to Yale. He wants to leave home. He wants to get away.

"Well, all I can say now is I'll think it over. But,

Robin, are you sure you know your own mind? You have the beach, you have a car here to drive when you need it, you have the club and your golf every day, and then there's Pamela. Who'll take Pamela to the dances Saturday nights?"

"Oh . . . Dad . . . let's be serious for once." He knew his father was joking. "Look, I have to know pretty soon. Butch wants me; he's holding off until you and Mother decide. But if I don't go, he'll get Mac or Bill Farmer."

"I still can't understand why you want to leave your home where everything is done for you . . ." The older man shook his head. Why does he ache so to leave the Point and the view out toward the Sound, where the harbor is filled with blue-tinted sailboats and the lights come on in Five Mile River every night and reflect and dance on the surface of the water? Why does he want to change this for the heat of the Middle West in midsummer? What does he see in that awful Morrison brat?

Now Robin began to be annoyed at his father. Usually Dad was understanding. Does he want to keep me here forever? I'm almost seventeen; I got my license last month. Being young is terrible. Whichever way you play it, you lose. You're Bob Longe's son, so everyone expects you to be a champion pole vaulter and captain of the track team and a cheerleader at the football games and a Bones man at Yale. If you can pole-vault and have money and go to Taft, people expect you to do the impossible and dislike you when you don't. If you have nothing, like Butch Morrison, they dislike you even worse. If you can't do a thing or play any sports, like Grimy Jackson at school, you're disliked too. How can you win? He sighed.

Then all the things he had been thinking and feeling and chewing over for months and months crystallized into one sentence. He almost threw the words across the porch at his father. "I want to be on my own."

The man whirled around and looked steadily at him. This remark stirred something deep in his own past. This trip of Robin's, this crazy idea, he realized now was not just a lark; it was not a sudden impulse on the boy's part. It was something that had been a deep part of him for a long, long time. It recalled his own feelings about his own father, who also had been a pole vaulter and Bones at Yale.

Glancing at the boy sitting there with the deep frown on his forehead, he saw that being young can be a tough period in a person's life. Most folks think of youth nostalgically as a wonderful time. Mine wasn't, he remembered. It wasn't all fun and good times by any means. There were many tough moments. So he listened with attention while the perplexed boy poured out his troubles.

"See now, Dad, you decide everything for me. Things are fine here, sure, but it's all too easy. You make the decisions. You tell me to take the College Boards. You say I'm going to Yale. O.K., I'm going. Only maybe I don't want to go to Yale. I can't explain how I feel, but I hate just being the same as you and Grandfather Longe. I don't want to be a pole vaulter at Yale. I want to get away with Butch . . . I'm old enough, Dad . . . I want to earn money . . ."

"How can you earn money? You've lived here every summer except when you were a kid and went to camp. You never held a job in your life. How on earth would you go about earning enough money to cross the continent? Just tell me that!"

"We'll pick up dough caddying at clubs along the way."

"Ha! You used to hate to caddie for me; you don't know the first thing about caddying now."

"Look, Dad, be reasonable, please. Anyone with two arms and two legs who plays golf can caddie. There's five thousand golf clubs in the United States; every club has jobs. Kids make big money, too, when they get doubles."

His father hesitated. "All right, tell you what. I won't say now you can go, but I promise I'll think it over carefully."

"Gee, Dad, you really mean that?"

"Yes, I mean it. I'll consider the thing carefully. I see your point of view. I remember how I felt at your age, and if you feel sure you want to leave perhaps you should. Maybe a few months away from home mightn't hurt you. But first of all we've got to sell your mother. You know as well as I do that'll be tough; she'll be dead against it."

Robin leaped up and hugged his father. The two of them together, he had discovered, could always win. But he was quickly shaken off. "No, no, Robin, this is a serious matter and I haven't fully made up my mind yet. I haven't had time to think this thing through. You'd have to promise me several things. First, you must promise you won't drink, not even beer. You'll have plenty of chances on the road."

"Oh, I promise, Dad, I promise. It's a promise."

"Then you must agree to write your mother at least twice a week. She'll be worrying the whole time you're gone. Those are only the first two promises I want to get over with you." He turned again and glanced out at the Sound. The blue-sailed yawl was merely a white wake in the distant dusk.

Maybe this might be an excellent thing, he was thinking. The boy would see a little of the country. After all, his whole life and his school have been around here. Perhaps when he returns he'll feel different about Yale. Most probably he'll get sick of the trip and come back in a week or ten days, anyhow. I remember how homesick I was on that ship to South America.

This is wonderful, this is great, it's turned out better than I expected, thought the boy. Dad's the kind of an old man to have; he understands things, he knows how a fellow feels. "Gee, Dad," he said, "you're really swell. You wait. You'll see. I'll write Mother twice a week."

"Another important point. If you go, I want everything settled at the start so we both know where we are. How much will this trip cost me?"

Robin stared at his father. Hadn't he explained already? "Cost you? Why, not a cent. I explained all that; we're earning our way. That's the whole point. You weren't listening, Dad."

"All right, all right, Robin. I'll start you off with twenty bucks, son, so you can eat the first few days. You can repay it when you return, if you want to. Now we must do a selling job on your mother. That's going to be tough."

Chapter 3

IT was next week when a 1937 convertible Ford drove around the circle before the house with a flourish, a roar, and an odor all its own. Pebbles scattered over the grass on both sides of the drive as the brakes moaned and the car scrunched to a stop. From an upper window Mrs. Longe observed that the car had certainly seen better days. There was a top, mostly in shreds. An ancient army tent, slightly green with mildew at the edges, covered some baggage in the rear.

A boy in jeans and checked shirt vaulted from the car with one hand. She saw that the door was wired on and probably expendable. To her, the car looked, smelled, and sounded like the town garbage truck which came around twice a week. However, she could see by the look on her son's face as he bounded out of the house that in reality this was a chariot straight from heaven.

Any last-minute hope she had had that he might still give up this mad attempt to cross the country in such a dilapidated machine died as she saw him rush up to the car.

"Hi, Whanger!"

"Hi, Torpo!"

Butch Morrison was slightly older than Robin, slightly heavier, slightly more experienced. In fact, a great deal more experienced, she guessed. Otherwise, she had to admit to herself, they were just two blond boys in dungarees and checked shirts, one the son of the town drunk, the other the son of the old Yale pole vaulter and New York advertising executive. You would have trouble telling one from the other.

She hated to go down, but somehow she had to face up to things. As she came out onto the grass, the two boys were shoving Robin's suitcase and golf bag under the army tent. Robin's father stood by attentively and when they had finished he took the boy aside and handed him an envelope.

"Here you are, son. Now pull up your socks!"

"Thanks lots, Dad, thanks. That's swell of you."

"Good morning, Mrs. Longe," said Butch Morrison. "Well, the big trek is about ready to get away. Hey there, Torpo!" He vaulted deftly onto the front seat and slid over behind the wheel. "C'mon, kid, let's get cracking!"

Robin's mother put her arms around him. "Robin-boy, do please be careful," she wanted to say. Instead she muttered feebly, "Well, if you boys feel you must leave, I suppose you must."

Robin kissed her and disengaged himself. "Yes'm. Yes, Mother, I guess we're really set now."

"Now remember, Robin!" She tried to be severe but it didn't quite come off. "Remember I do not want you going without regular meals. Or eating cokes and hot dogs instead of decent food."

"But what's wrong with cokes and hot dogs?" he wanted to ask. However, he refrained. It seemed wise not to get into an argument at that particular moment.

Robin went over to his father. They always kissed each other when either of them was leaving on a trip of any length. So, even with Butch eying him impatiently from the front seat, Robin made the concession to sentiment and custom. Although it was difficult to imagine Butch kissing Old Man Morrison at any time.

He skipped joyfully around to the side of the car, climbed up over the door held together by wire, jumped into the seat. The motor roared like a B34. Vast columns of smoke filled the air with a poisonous odor.

His father waved. "Take it easy now," he shouted above the roar of the engine. His mother managed a smile.

The car jerked forward suddenly, swirled dangerously around the little circle scattering pebbles onto the grass to right and left. They turned into Sound View Avenue and the world lay before them.

This was it. They were off at last. He was Vasco da Gama leaving Portugal, he was Columbus climbing aboard the *Pinta,* he was Pizarro and La Salle and Père Marquette. Before them stretched the open road, unknown country. To be sure, it was only Route 104 going across the state line into New York; but to Robin it was adventure, it was freedom. Ahead was romance. Behind was pole-vault practice and requests not to be late for dinner. He could have shouted with joy. The sun shone; it was a perfect June morning. Presently he did shout. Butch joined in, feeling the spirit of the moment too. He was the ideal companion.

Soon they were out of Connecticut and into New York. Butch was an excellent driver. He had quick reflexes and good co-ordination; he handled the ancient Ford like a master. On the whole, however, Robin was glad his parents were not along as they wove in and out of traffic, roaring past bigger cars, their exhaust smoking. At eleven they stopped for gas. A check showed they also needed oil.

"Now, that's funny. I had it filled up last night. This bus sure eats the oil," sighed Butch. "Hey, Torpo, I'm hungry. How about eats?"

Robin was hungry also. They went inside to a counter and ordered cokes and hot dogs. The food tasted good, yet somehow Robin had a guilty feeling as he ate.

The first golf course they passed in the Catskills

had a dozen couples on it, and every one was followed by caddies. They decided to skip it. The next,
fifteen miles along, astonished them by needing no
help. Butch conducted all negotiations, returning
from the pro shop annoyed and surprised. When the
third club also had plenty of caddies, they looked
at each other in dismay.

"Say! When we gonna land a job?" said Robin.
"I thought all golf clubs needed caddies."

"Relax, Torpo. We'll grab one off tomorrow.
Trouble is, this is a resort region. There's caddie
camps around here."

"Caddie camps, what's that?"

"Camps where they train caddies. When the clubs
around phone in and say how many caddies they
want that morning, the camp sends 'em over by
bus."

They moved along, weaving in and out of traffic
at no slow speed. It gave Robin a pleasantly exhilarated feeling. He felt sure his mother would have
disapproved of Butch's driving. Then his companion spoke. "That Pamela Griswold there at the
club, she's some doll," he remarked.

Robin grunted. Somehow he felt reluctant to discuss her with Butch, who immediately tried another
topic.

"This-here school you go to . . . what's it
called?"

"Taft."

"Yeah. Whad'you guys do there, anyway?"

"We work," replied Robin, with emphasis.

"Work?" said Butch, in an outraged tone.

"Sure do. Recitations eight to one . . ."

"Recitations?"

"Classes, see. Then we have assembly and lunch; then pole vaulting until four-thirty; then study until vespers, and study after dinner in the evening, too."

"Don't you do anything but study?"

"Oh, yes. When I was a kid in Lower Middle, we built a hockey rink."

At last Butch was impressed. "No kidding!"

"That's right. We really did—three hundred of us; we worked all winter. The kids laid eight and a half miles of pipe. We painted and laid out the fences . . . say . . . What's that? That noise?"

An ominous knocking sounded, died away, sprang to life violently again, and continued. Robin felt uneasy as the noise kept on, and a glance at Butch's face told him that Butch was worried too. Now what? Suppose the old bus breaks down. Suppose we have to quit and go back when we've only just got under way!

Butch steered the car off on the grass at the side of the road, jumped out, and opened the hood. "H'm . . . I see . . . I see," he muttered, taking some tools from the rear. It was impossible not to have confidence in him, for apparently he understood the car's insides perfectly and how to restore them to health. He fumbled with the engine, Robin standing helpless at one side.

"Gimme that wrench! No, not that one, the pipe wrench, stupid. How can I get at this nut with an ordinary monkey wrench?"

Robin handed him the tool. He worked away rapidly and calmly, master of himself and the engine. In five minutes he vaulted into the seat, started the engine again, and listened attentively. No noise, no knocking, nothing.

"Gee, Butch, you're something, you really are," said Robin as he climbed in. There was envy in his feeling and there was admiration also; surely Butch was the perfect companion on the open road.

Butch accepted the tribute casually. "Yeah, you gotta know this old bus. She ain't no Cadillac."

Robin said nothing. He felt slightly ashamed because his father drove a Cadillac.

At two-thirty they passed a driving range. Butch cut in on a sudden impulse and climbed out of the car. The boss, a swarthy, disagreeable man in a white coat and a faded straw hat, was behind a counter in a small shed. Golf clubs leaning against the counter and piles of balls in tin buckets were awaiting the clients.

Robin sat for quite a while in the car as Butch and the man argued. Finally they emerged from the little shed, and the man took Butch by the arm and pointed down the road. Butch vaulted into the front seat. "He claims he can only give us sixty-five cents an hour. Says that's what he pays regularly, the old cheat. It's slave labor, that's what it is, but it's the best I could do. He owns a field two miles down the road. Says we can put the tent up there."

They found the field with no trouble, pitched the tent where it could not be seen from the road, and returned to the driving range, Butch still complaining about the pay. They parked the car and got out. At one side was a tractor covered with wire as a protection from flying golf balls. Butch instantly climbed in, started it, and was off onto the field while Robin stood watching. The machine scooped up stray balls with the driver entirely shielded. Robin, on the other hand, had to go out and pick up balls by hand, with no protection whatever.

Business was somewhat slow at first. Then it improved around five o'clock as people returned from work. At six, the two went back to the tent and unpacked their supplies; Robin cooked bacon and eggs and they drank milk. There was no time to wash the dishes. 818265

On their return to the range, Butch went over to the tractor and had started to get inside when a big fellow came running over and pulled him away. "That's not for you, Mac. That's my job."

Butch turned around belligerently, ready for a scrap.

The owner noticed it and shouted, "That tractor's

Tommy's. That's his machine. He's my regular night man. Get out there and shag balls and don't start trouble, young fella."

Butch looked at the big fellow and then looked out at the field. "I should go out there and get killed for sixty-five cents an hour," he muttered.

The man spoke up again. "Wait a minute. Come on in here awhile and hand out these balls. You can make change as well as I can." With that he summoned Butch into the little shed with the tin pails of golf balls on the counter.

Robin returned to the business of picking up balls in the field. As dusk deepened and the lights went on, this became a hazardous undertaking. Golf balls whizzed and screamed past his head, and he began to dislike the work intensely. This was not caddying as he had anticipated it—carrying golf bags in daylight and on a pleasant fairway for agreeable gentlemen who gave you large tips. This was murder. However, he stuck it out until midnight, when business fell off and the boss called him in and paid them both—with reluctance, it appeared. For their work he gave them exactly five dollars and twenty cents apiece.

"See you tomorrow, fellas," he called as they drove away.

"I knew the guy was a crook," remarked Butch. "I told you so."

"Five bucks for risking your life all evening. That's grim."

"Yeah, you had it really ·tough. I got to him, though. I took the chiseler. I took him all right." He held up a ten-dollar bill.

At first Robin did not get the implication. Slowly he realized that Butch had presided over the cash register most of the evening and had found a chance to pocket a ten-dollar bill. Before he could stop himself he had mumbled, "No! You mean . . . you took it?"

"Sure. Why not? If a guy tries to get funny with Butch Morrison, he's fooling with the wrong guy."

Robin was shocked. He had to admit that once or twice there had been fellows at school who stole. But this was worse; this was done in such cold blood that it rocked him. You couldn't believe it, yet you had to. Butch had even boasted about it. Somehow he suddenly became a far less desirable companion than he had seemed that morning.

Rain began to fall. Robin felt cold, tired, unhappy. This thing would be between them all through their journey, across the entire country. Not for the first time that evening, he wished he was in his comfortable bed at home. Butch honked angrily at a car ahead, a black sedan going along at about thirty-five miles an hour, square in the middle of the road. Again the horn sounded with vigor. Butch was tired too, and consequently impatient.

The sedan still hugged the center, so Butch pounded the horn once more and swung out to pass it. As soon as he was ahead he slowed down and gently forced the sedan off to the side. It was a dangerous maneuver, Robin felt, holding tight to the side of the car.

In a minute Butch speeded up and they were off down the road. Before they reached their camping spot, however, a horrible sound came from behind. It was unmistakably the siren of a police car. Butch had shoved a state cop off the road!

Robin's training at home and at school had taught him a decent respect for authority. Not so Butch. Stopping the car, he leaned back as the cop stepped out of the black sedan behind them and slowly came up. "Whatcha mean staying out in the middle of the road like that? I couldn't get past ya."

The policeman ignored the remark, merely holding out his hand. "Let's see your license." He took it, bent over, a flashlight in his hand. Then he turned the light on the two boys and held it there. "Where you kids from?"

"Five Mile River, Connecticut, like it says there."

"Where you going?"

"Out West. We're caddying at golf clubs. We're looking for jobs."

"Dontcha know better'n to run me off the road like that? You could catch a fender, then where are you? I'll tell you. Your friend is out on the pavement with a broken skull. You're probably wrapped around a telephone pole. You crazy, son?" It was a grim suggestion. Even Butch had no glib rejoinder. "I oughta run you two guys in. Now get moving, and next time don't get fresh and try any funny business, young fella, hear me? The boys up ahead will all be watching for you."

He stood copying their license numbers. Then he returned the licenses to Butch and went back to his car. They moved quickly away.

"How was I to know it was a state cop? Those guys make me sick. They hog the road and then try to blame you for it."

The rain was coming down faster now. When they turned into their field, the grass was soggy and wet. The tent, pitched on low ground, had to be moved. By the time they finished they were both hot, wet, exhausted, for even with the help of the car lights the job took time.

Flies buzzed around the dirty plates in the dampness. "We oughta clean these dishes tonight, Butch."

"Tomorrow. I'll do it tomorrow morning. I'm all in now. Doesn't your back ache, picking up those balls all over that jerk's driving range? Mine does, just watching you."

"Why, no," Robin replied, realizing that at times pole vaulting had its advantages. He crawled into the low army tent, yanked off his clothes, and tucked himself into a blanket. It was hot, damp, sticky. The rain, now a downpour, was leaking under the sides of the tent. A million mosquitoes swarmed around, and he had to keep his head under the blanket to keep from being eaten up.

Somehow both his companion and the open road seemed very different now from the moment when he and Butch had left Five Mile River in the sunshine a few hours and a few miles before. It seemed years away.

Chapter 4

"BUT looka here, Butch! You got oil just yesterday—two quarts. You filled her up then, remember?"

"I know I did, kid. This old bus sure drinks oil. Can't help it."

Robin did some quick figuring. Now he became really worried. Gas and oil were running into money, and he couldn't help wondering whether the old car would be able to get them across the country, let alone bring them back. He felt it was fortunate they had both nailed down a job at last.

That morning they had stopped at a luxurious golf and country club on the outskirts of Utica, and had been immediately hired as caddies. Once again, and not for the last time, Robin remembered his father's remarks, for he soon discovered there was more to caddying than he suspected, that indeed he knew little about it. At first he made many mistakes and was called down for them, too, but by evening he had earned eight dollars and felt better. Butch, who was quick, aggressive, and used to caddying, picked up ten dollars. So, in spite of the expenses for gas and oil, they were jubilant as they drove to a field where the pro had told them they could camp. They pitched the tent near a small stream.

Robin washed in the stream, and after their usual meal of peanut-butter sandwiches, bacon and eggs, and milk, he began slowly to clean things up. Twice a week at home, when Fanny was not there, he helped with the dishes. But slipping plates and silverware into a dishwasher and cleaning them in a cold stream of running water are two very different things. Butch had cooked the meal so, according to their agreement, Robin had to clean up afterward.

"Hey there, Torpo," Butch called out presently, "I could go for a beer. What say we run down the road a ways and then fix this mess up when we come back? I'll help you. We'll polish it off in no time."

"Aw, Whanger, it'll be dark when we get back."

"No matter, I'll do it. Let's drive down to that tavern and have a quick one."

Reluctantly Robin climbed in beside him and they went down the highway a few miles, where Butch turned in at a tavern with the sign, *Joe and Mac. Beer and Ale*. They parked the car and went inside.

The place was like a million other such places throughout the land—a long bar, half a dozen booths, some tables in the center of the room. The light was dim, the floor dirty. But Robin felt it was a romantic spot. At school he had sneaked off with the seniors one night and gone to a tavern in Waterbury, all the time feeling nervous and uncomfortable. There was little chance to visit taverns at home, because Five Mile River had no license. So this one was especially interesting to him.

The bartender, an enormous man with a face like a seal, came toward them, wiping the counter. He looked at each one intently for a moment, saying nothing.

"Two beers," said Butch, with the air of a man to whom taverns were old stuff. "Schlitz." The bartender didn't move. He stood looking at them hard, his arms on the counter. "How old are you two?"

"Eighteen."

"Ya don't look it. I ain't losing my license for a coupla kids, no, sir. This-here boy eighteen?"

Robin felt uncomfortable at being singled out in this manner. "I really don't want beer. I'd rather have a coke," he interjected feebly.

"Oh, c'mon, Torpo. Don't let this guy getcha down. Have a beer."

Men along the bar leaned over to listen and look at them. "No, thanks. I'll stick to cokes tonight." Robin felt unwilling to mention the promise he had made his father before leaving.

The bartender grunted, moved away, and returned with a beer and a bottle of coke. Robin paid quickly.

Butch lit a cigarette. "Let's us sit down at a table and be comfortable. What say, kid?"

They took the glasses and moved to one of the tables. Slowly the tavern was filling up. Most of the customers were watching a ball game on the television set at one end of the bar. This, Robin felt, was seeing life. At last he was on his own and doing what he wanted to do. By now, at home, his mother would have begun to hint that if he was going to get to the club for that match at ten the next morning, it was time for him to go to bed. Actually, he had never felt more awake or more alive.

Butch drank his beer, rose, and soon returned to the table with another bottle. He gulped with evident pleasure. "Have some?" he said, holding up the bottle. "It's good, Torpo. It's really cold."

"No, thanks. Beer and coke don't mix."

"Yeah, I guess. Looka there!"

Everyone turned to the screen. The voice of the announcer rose in a kind of frenzy. "It's . . . it's . . . it is . . . yes . . . it's going . . . it's going . . . it's gone! It's a grand-slam homer . . . a grand slammer for Casey. And that ties the score, folks, five to five."

Two sailors came in with pretty girls and sat at the table next to the boys. The place was getting livelier and a hum rose over the room. Everyone seemed to be laughing and having a good time. Unquestionably an exciting life, this, and Robin was grateful to Butch for getting him away and taking him into the world. Except for Butch, he would be sitting quietly on the porch at home, watching the Rands' yacht steam through the harbor entrance for an evening on the Sound, or calling Pamela Griswold on the telephone.

"Say! I seen your old man at the club last week. He had on a blue sweater with a white *Y* on it, turned inside out. He was a jumper or something at Yale, wasn't he?"

Robin would have preferred to discuss Butch's father, a vastly more entertaining figure, who had once worked in a circus. But you couldn't exactly say, "One night after the movies last week I saw your old man coming out of Finnegan's. He could walk." Therefore he merely grunted.

Butch, however, kept on. "What for does he wear his sweater inside out, Torpo?"

"I dunno. Likes it that way, I guess. Or maybe he just didn't notice." This was a subtle problem to get across. He did know why. Even at Taft, where he was captain of the track team, Robin seldom wore his sweater right side out. But it was difficult to explain.

Fortunately, at this moment Butch was seized with the desire for another drink. He rose and went to the bar. Robin hoped they would refuse to serve him; but another bartender had come on who didn't notice, and he whipped up the beer in a hurry.

Butch returned, sat down, and announced in loud tones, "Well, tomorrow's another day. Let's hope we have some real luck for a change. Here's to good old Yale, Torpo-kid." He thumped the bottle on the table and raised his glass.

The sailors and their girls eyed him curiously. People nearby turned around. Robin became less certain that this business of seeing life was entirely fun.

The beer was half consumed. Butch's capacity seemed endless. He turned to Robin. "Have another coke?"

"No, thanks; no, thanks. Don't you think maybe we better get going?" It was probably the first time in his life he had ever wanted to get to bed.

"Whassa hurry?" Butch demanded in loud tones. "Tomorrow's Saturday. I'm gonna knock down twenty bucks, what with the tips and all. One guy spoke for me already."

Robin was impressed. Then, with no warning, Butch suddenly broke into song.

"Aw, skip it, Whanger; skip it, please. That big guy behind the bar is watching us. He'll get mad if you don't pipe down." Robin was embarrassed. He hated the whole thing; for now they were beginning to be noticed. Even the row of men leaning over their glasses at the bar were turning around with wide smiles.

"What of it? What if he is looking at us?" Butch was really addressing the sailors and their girls at the adjoining table. "I gotta right here." He went on singing and his voice, rising higher, could be heard above the hum and buzz of conversation and the voice of the television announcer. The couples at the next table were vastly amused, even applauding him at this point.

All at once, to Robin's dismay, Butch broke into another song. "Raise . . . a stein . . . for dear old Yale. . . ."

"No . . . no, Butch, not Yale. It's Maine, not Yale." Robin tried hard to quiet him down, uncomfortable at the attention being paid them and also with an uneasy feeling he had the good name of Yale to protect. Somehow there was a responsibility on him. Fortunately, his father was not along to see the proceedings, he thought.

Butch was now really enjoying himself. "C'mon, Torpo-kid. C'mon, have a beer. You gotta be a big Yale man like your dad, Torpo."

Everyone in the tavern was watching with interest, and Robin could hear comments from all sides. "Coupla college students." Not for the first time that evening he began to long for the peaceful porch overlooking Five Mile River, with nothing but the sound of boats returning from an evening on the Sound.

Butch rose. He held out his arms. Then he picked up his glass. "C'mon, folks, everybody sing. Let every loyal son of Yale . . ."

"No, Butch, it isn't Yale. It's Maine. That's the Maine *Stein Song;* it has nothing to do with Yale. Sit down, Whanger, sit down, please sit down."

Butch refused to subside. The whole room was his audience and he was enjoying it. He stood bowing to a slight ripple of applause from the sailors and their girls at the next table. Then he put his glass down and started to step up on his chair. At that moment he was seized from behind, one hand grasping his collar, one the seat of his trousers.

Robin had to admire the ease and skill with which the big bartender propelled Butch across the room. One energetic shove through the open door, and he was stumbling and falling into the road outside.

Chastened, red-faced, thoroughly ashamed of himself and his pal, Robin quickly followed.

"And don't ever come back, ya hear?" said the bartender, as he closed the door with a bang.

Butch snored loudly. Robin felt that school, where there were stout-nosed snorers and snorters, had made him an authority on the subject. Yet never had he listened to such noises as his companion made after their return from the tavern. Twice Butch rose to stick his head out of the tent and retch violently.

Yet he never appeared to be conscious, and sank at once into a loud series of grunts and groans.

Miserable and unhappy, uncomfortable in mind and body, Robin lay awake, listening to the noises of his companion, to the rain spatter on the side of the tent, miserable and unhappy. When Butch struggled out for the second time, he made his decision. This was enough. It wouldn't work, he realized. He disliked admitting that his mother had been right in her estimate of Butch. Difficult as it was to face, however, the fact was plain. Butch was not the pal he wanted to go along with on a cross-country trip.

What decided him was not the theft at the driving range, although as he lay there he could not get the thought of it out of his mind. It wasn't that, although Robin knew this would be between them through their entire journey. It was not the scene in the tavern or Butch's fondness for beer. It was all of these things together and other things he hardly understood. Butch simply was not the same. He had become a different person since they left Five Mile River.

Robin lay there wide awake, his hands behind his head, thinking hard. It was a long time since he had thought like this. What next? If he was to break away and leave, he must get off early and avoid a scene. The next step was less clear, yet there were but two choices: go back home and admit the whole idea had been a wretched mistake, or go on alone. It didn't take him long to choose.

Day came, a dank, sodden morning, as disagreeable as Robin's unhappy thoughts. Butch was still snoring and presumably would go on for the rest of the morning. Robin rose and surveyed the dirty dishes. This was his job, so he went down to the creek, washed them in cold water, dried them carefully, and piled them just inside the tent. He packed his suitcase, took his golf bag, and sat down in the car to write two of the most difficult letters he had ever composed.

Half a dozen scribbled starts were thrown away. Perhaps, he thought, the shortest and simplest message was the best. Butch was on the ball; he would understand.

Dear Butch,
    After thinking things over this morning, I've decided to go on alone. Good luck.

                                        Torpo.

He stuffed the note into the pocket of Butch's trousers. Then he took it out again and put it in one of Butch's shoes, weighting it down with a rock.

Next came the harder letter of the two, yet it also had to be written.

Dear Mother,
    I find you were right about Butch and I was wrong.

Then came a long period of thought. It hurt to write those words, but what else could he say?

> I've decided to go on alone, so please don't worry. I've had several golf jobs already and have some money. Will wire you where you can write me. Love to you and Dad.
>
> Robin.

He slipped the letter into a stamped and addressed envelope his mother had provided him with, put it in his coat pocket, took up his suitcase and golf bag. It would have been much easier, he now realized, had he left his clubs at home. Also it would have been simpler had he gone off alone; easier still had he never started.

He put the idea out of his mind and lugged his bags through the muddy field to the side of the highway. This is it, he thought. I wanted to be on my own; now I really am.

Chapter 5

LOOKING back, Robin recalled listening at school to disputes about hitchhiking—which side of a traffic light you should stand on, just how to point or wave, what to say to a cop who stopped you. These discussions were far away and unreal, for he had never paid much attention. Now he wished he had listened and learned. It was always like that; you paid no attention in a class, you sat thinking about the meet Saturday, or some girl coming to a tea dance during the week end, and then suddenly the College Boards were on top of you. And you didn't have some of the answers you needed.

He vaguely remembered hearing that some states have laws against hitchhiking. Was New York one? He would soon find out. Feebly he held out his right arm. It was an unconvincing gesture and he knew it.

Whoosh . . . whoosh . . . whoosh! The cars flashed by him in an endless stream.

Unquestionably his mother had been right all the

time about Butch. Hang it, she *had* been right; it hurt to admit it, yet it was true. There is surely nothing in the world harder than having to face up to the fact that your parents were right and knew more than you did. Unless it is having to set the fact down on paper.

Whoosh . . . whoosh . . . whoosh . . . whoosh went the Buicks and Fords and Pontiacs. Whoosh . . . whoosh . . . whoosh!

He stood there with his hand held out indecisively. The cars whizzing past finally made him dizzy, or else it was the fact that he was without breakfast. He turned his head a few minutes and then turned back. The Chryslers and Cadillacs were still roaring past at sixty or better, it seemed. Whoosh . . . whoosh . . . whoosh!

He stood trying to smile, finding it difficult to smile on an empty stomach in the rain at such an early hour. The cars kept rolling past, their windshield wipers moving, nobody anxious to pick up a hatless boy with a suitcase and golf bag at the side of the road. After twenty long minutes with no result, Robin realized that hitchhiking was by no means as easy as it sounded. He began to see that he would never catch a ride at that spot. Somehow he must get to a traffic light or a crossroads, some place where cars were slowing down. Of course, he could walk back a mile to the tavern, but that place had unhappy associations and he decided to push on.

Picking up his bag and golf clubs, he started walking. Instantly an annoyed squawk came from behind; then another and another, as each car edged toward the center of the highway yet spattered him with water at the same time. Hang it, he thought, these road hogs want the entire highway. For the first time he saw automobiles from a different viewpoint. It soon became apparent that he must walk on the other side.

But he had to keep well off the concrete to avoid being hit. The grass was wet, the footing soft and soggy, his bags heavy. Consequently progress was hard and slow. Rain trickled down over his face, carried perspiration into his eyes and his mouth. It was necessary to watch every step, because one slip could tumble him into the path of the oncoming motors.

Finally, after half an hour's slow walking, he saw a neon light ahead on the other side of the road. When he reached the place he discovered it was a diner and immediately crossed over. He was hungry. He counted his cash, twenty-six dollars and a few pennies—to take him across the continent.

However, after a good breakfast he had dried off a little and felt better. A dozen cars were parked outside the diner, and as soon as he finished eating, Robin went outside and stood waiting, studying his road map and looking up the towns ahead. Whenever anybody came out to his car, Robin spoke up.

"Not going toward Syracuse, are you?" "Not going west, are you, Mister?"

Perhaps this was the wrong approach. Most of the drivers paid no attention at all or shook their heads. A few stated that they were headed back the other way. After another half hour the line of cars parked around the diner thinned out, and he was in despair. Truly this hitchhiking was tough. Fellows made it sound so easy; you stood on the road with your thumb out until somebody stopped and took you to your exact destination. It didn't seem to be working out that way. The way it worked out was that you stood several hours in a downpour, got soaking wet, and no ride.

Probably right now the sun is shining in Five Mile River, he thought gloomily, sparkling on the Sound. I could be out sailing with Pamela at this minute instead of being here in this mess.

Just then a big bus marked *Albany* drew in for a short stop. Robin felt sure he had enough cash for bus fare home, and his impulse was to climb aboard.

But I can't give up like that, he thought. That's just what they expected me to do. I got myself in this and I've got to stick with it. If I go back, he thought, I'll have to do exactly what they want from here on in.

So he watched the bus slosh out onto the road, the passengers, dry and comfortable, eying him curiously from the windows. He was almost relieved to see it disappear in the distance, he wanted so badly to get on it.

A few minutes later a small delivery truck slithered in and came to a stop. The driver, in a long white coat, alighted, went to the rear of the truck, yanked out a set of trays containing pies and cakes, and entered the diner. He was inside ten minutes. When he reappeared there were fewer cakes and pies on the various trays.

"Not going toward Syracuse, are you?" asked Robin mechanically.

"Syracuse?" The man in the coat hesitated, his arms full of trays. "Why, no, son. I'm only going part ways toward Rome. That do you any good?"

"You bet." He grabbed his two bags and stowed them away in the rear between the trays of food. He felt elated. The fact of sitting up there with the man in the white coat gave him a terrific lift, for this was his first ride, perhaps his only ride. Yet at least he had stayed with the thing until the ride came along. This proved you could do it—if you would only stick it out.

Sitting there, he felt like an emperor as they drew out onto the road. He glanced at his watch and immediately his elation vanished. It was after ten-thirty. At this rate it would take a month to get to California.

The driver's name was Tom Sweeney, so the plate

on the dash said. Robin soon learned that his job was to deliver cakes and pies and to pick up the two-day-old ones and turn them back to a bakery near Rome.

Sweeney dropped him on the outskirts of the city, and once again Robin was on his own. He walked toward a traffic light and began the dismal business all over again. How many times, he wondered, will I have to do this before I see home again?

When the light was red, the cars squeaked to a stop and the drivers looked indifferently at the be-draggled figure on the curb, then moved along as soon as the signal changed. When the light was green, the drivers never noticed him at all. Before long he began to feel dizzy once more as the cars whizzed endlessly past. After half an hour his arm ached and his eyes were weary. He turned, to break the monot-ony of that endless stream, unfastened his golf bag, took a driver, and whipped it several times through the air. The exercise loosened him up a little. Step-ping aside, he swung the driver once more, and felt his tension ease.

But as he turned back, the Dodges and Nashes were still going past in that endless procession—whoosh . . . whoosh . . . whoosh!

This was evidently not a good spot to pick up a ride. But what was a good spot, he wondered, as he stood leaning on the driver and pointing with his hand. His whole bearing was hopeless and negative, as if he didn't really expect to get a ride.

A car suddenly screeched to a stop five hundred feet ahead. Just as suddenly, it started to back up to the spot where Robin stood at the side of the road, his mouth open.

"Jump in, son." The man spoke as if he was used to giving orders. Robin leaped. Without waiting to slam the driver into the golf bag, he threw his suitcase and clubs into the rear of the car and climbed into the front seat, holding the driver in his hand.

"Gee, thanks lots, Mister. Thanks lots." How lovely the road looked from the front seat of a Chrysler Imperial! To himself he vowed never to pass anyone on the road again without giving him a lift. He sank back into the cushions and glanced at the driver. About forty, Robin thought, brisk, competent, good-looking; in some ways he resembled Dad.

"What's your name, son?" said the man. "Mine's Haskell."

"Robin Longe," mumbled Robin. "And thanks a lot for picking me up. This rain is no fun."

The man laughed genially. "I don't pick up hikers as a rule, but when I saw you swinging that club I just couldn't resist. Guess you're a golfer too."

"Yes, sir," said Robin, still panting from excitement. "Least I hope I will be some day."

The man laughed. He had a most engaging smile. "Don't we all! Where you headed for?"

"West."

"West? That covers a mighty lot of territory, boy. What part of the West?"

"California, I guess."

"California! Well, you've got some territory ahead, haven't you? But you're lucky. This is Friday and I'm due home in Evanston tomorrow. That'll get you as far as Chicago. How you been doing, had any trouble hitching rides?"

"Sometimes. It all depends," he answered truthfully.

"I never pick up strangers, never. Too dangerous nowadays. But seeing your golf bag and all, I couldn't help myself. Your old man play?"

"Yes, sir. He plays."

"I suppose he taught you, didn't he?"

"Why, yes and no. I mean, I guess so. See now, he's interested in all sports, sailing and everything."

"Oh. Where's he play golf?"

"Sweet Briar."

"Sweet Briar! Wait a minute. That's . . . I know where that is. That's in Connecticut some place, isn't it?" Robin nodded. "Sure. Our New York district manager plays there. He lives out that way. What d'you shoot, son?"

"Oh . . . my best score is 79. But I'm usually around 82 or 83."

"I'd sure like to break 80. Can't get under 85 to save my life. I play Skokie. I'd give money to be able to hit 79 there. Tough course, Skokie. They've played the Open there and all the pros complain. Say it's the hardest layout they ever saw."

So it went. Robin discovered he didn't need to say much; he could just nod and ask a question now and then about his host's game. Into Niagara Falls and over the border. Along the Queen Elizabeth Highway, he learned that Mr. Haskell laid them right to the pin from fifty feet with a six iron, the club he liked best. Across the farms and orchards of Ontario, Robin heard the story of how much he had won at the dollar Nassau the week before. At Windsor they came back again into the United States. To the man at the wheel, who kept discussing his golf, this was all routine, for he had done it many times. To Robin, who had never before crossed his country's frontier, it was an exciting experience.

When they stopped in Detroit for dinner, it was almost six o'clock. Robin would have preferred a lunch wagon to save money, but his friend steered him to a hotel where the parking would be easier. During the meal Mr. Haskell said, "I s'pose you're on the golf team at school if you shoot a 79."

"Well . . . not exactly . . . no. I have no time for golf at school. Fact is, I'm on the track team."

"Ah, you're a runner. I should have known that.

You've got the build of a runner, long and rangy. What distance?"

"No, sir, I'm a pole vaulter. I don't run except once in a while when someone is laid up. I jump and do the pole."

"That so! We had a pole vaulter in college; one of the best in the country he was, too." The man suddenly stopped, put down his fork, looked searchingly across the table. "Young fella, what did you say your name was?"

"Robin Longe."

"Not Longe with an *E*."

He nodded. "Yessir."

"Why, then you must be related to Bob Longe, the old Yale pole vaulter."

It made Robin feel warm all over. "Why, that's my old man," he said. "That's my dad."

Mr. Haskell shoved his chair back. "Well, for heaven's sake! To think I'd pick you up, of all people. It's a small world after all, isn't it? Why, Bob Longe was in the class ahead of me. I knew him well. I didn't recognize your name. When you said your name, Robin . . ."

"Yes, sir, my name isn't really Robin. I was named for my dad. I'm Robert B. Longe, Third. But he's always been called Bob, so when I was a baby Mother started calling me Robin, and around home it stuck. Kids at school . . . they don't know . . . most everyone there calls me Bob."

"Well, well, sure enough. Think of it, my picking you up like this. Are you as good at the pole as your old man? How high d'you get? I presume you're headed for Yale." Mr. Haskell took the check and shoved Robin's money aside. "From Bob Longe's boy? Certainly not."

Robin knew enough about Yale men not to deny the suggestion about his ending at New Haven. "Thanks a lot, sir. Yes, I really hope to get to college some day. I get around twelve-six or so. It takes a lot of practice. I like golf, myself," he added, as they went out of the dining room.

"I see, I understand. Of course you'll be on the track team at New Haven. Now tell you what—you're going to stay here at the hotel tonight as my guest, and we'll just get your father on long distance and let you talk to him. I'd enjoy talking to him myself. Haven't seen him since the last reunion."

Chapter 6

AT Skokie, Robin received something of a shock. There was, he soon discovered, far more to caddying than he had ever suspected. In fact, he realized that his father had been right. Although Robin had spent much time with Butch and the other caddies at Sweet Briar, he really knew nothing about the job and had never actually lugged bags for money except that afternoon at Utica.

He soon began to learn. That a caddie is expected to be an amateur meteorologist, a psychologist, an authority on the course with a complete knowledge of the rules of the game. He must know all the local hazards, how wind affects various shots, what lies behind the green and what doesn't. That was only the start of it.

When you were caddying, he found, you could not relax a second or someone snarled at you. You had to be ready to tee up the ball, hand out the correct club, stand in the proper place, watch that drive fade into the distance, and then lead your player to it. Some members were agreeable, some were not.

The latter growled and groused when they were off their game or made mistakes. Mistakes often were blamed on the caddie. The country club was no longer a pleasant place with friendly, smiling men around. Here he was a number, not a member and the son of a member. For the first time he saw a country club from the outside in, not from the inside out.

Much of this he felt the moment Mr. Haskell introduced him to Sandy Ferguson, the club pro at Skokie. The man greeted him politely but with no enthusiasm whatever, eying him curiously, looking him up and down, nodding. "Why, yes. Yes, Mr. Haskell, we can use the young man. Jim! This is Bob Longe, friend of Mr. Haskell's. Jim Henry's our caddie master. You can work him in, can't you, Jim?"

The caddie master was a young man, tall and thin. He looked overworked. He introduced Robin to a boy about his own age named Mac, one of the veteran caddies. Mac asked him if he knew golf and the rules, assuming he had caddied before and understood his duties. In a general way, he did. There were, however, many things to learn and now there was only one way of learning them—the hard way.

Everything here was new and different. Nobody smiled at him; no one was friendly. The members spoke to him quickly and sharply, their minds on the next shot. They expected him to jump when they did speak. The first few days he spent shagging balls, tedious and boring work, or chasing around with old men in endless foursomes that every other caddie evaded. He did not enjoy what happened at the end of the day when the caddie master frisked him carefully to be sure he was not hiding any balls. The first time it happened he resented this; then when the caddie master did it to the others, too, he understood and took it for what it was—part of the job.

The second afternoon he spent with Sandy Ferguson, who was giving lessons. His task was to chase balls. Once he returned to the pro, who stood on the practice field with a lady pupil, and emptied the bag of balls at his feet. He had turned to go back when the pro spoke sharply. "Here, wait a minute! Twenty . . . twenty-one . . . twenty-two . . . that right? Yes, twenty-two. That all you got? There's four missing, young fella. I think they're out to the left. You're paid to watch those balls; that's what you're there for. Now go back and find 'em; they're in the long grass to the left, all four."

Sure enough, they were, too. After this he returned to the pro with the bag full.

Skokie was a bigger and more luxurious Sweet Briar. Robin found out that it was not just a wooden lattice that separated him from the laughing boys and girls on the clubhouse porch. These girls, with names like Patricia and Camilla and Penelope, these boys, who went to Eastern prep schools and drove

Jaguars and M.G.'s, were in a different world. In Robin's world you jumped when someone spoke to you, and men frisked you every night after work.

But before long Robin began to get the hang of caddying. It was no longer strange when someone addressed him abruptly as "Boy," or spoke sharply to him on the tee. The good caddie, he realized, is a fine piece of equipment. He knows the course, the distance between holes, and exactly where the worst traps are placed. He never tells the player what club to use but pulls out several different irons for his choice. The good caddie is on the job every minute.

Sometimes this was not easy. Over the week end the course was crowded, all the caddies were kept busy, and he spent two long days out on the fairways, lugging heavy bags in a torrid Midwestern heat wave. Saturday evening he finished late, and while waiting for a ride into town with one of the caddies who had a car, he stood at the back of the clubhouse, watching the dinner dance through the windows. Inside was a girl with hair on her shoulders, who resembled Pam Griswold. She was dancing with a boy about his own age. Pamela, he had always been sure, was the most attractive girl in the world; he was not so sure now. He wanted to be in there dancing cheek to cheek with that pretty blonde girl. I belong there, he thought angrily.

"Hey, there, fella, you coming?"

The caddie's yell brought him out of his dream,

and with reluctance he turned away. They would be dancing tonight at Sweet Briar, too, and he suddenly wondered with whom Pamela was dancing.

On Sunday afternoon, late, he saw that at last he had drawn an agreeable human being, a man who didn't take himself or his game too seriously. He stood waggling his club on the first tee. He stepped off and took several practice swings. At last he addressed the ball once more. He raised and lowered the driver several times, shook his muscles loose, sighted off into the distance in preparation for a tremendous drive. Then he hauled off and hit the ball a miserable thirty yards or so, out to the right and into the rough.

Behind him, the other men grinned silently. The man on the tee straightened up, looked around, and remarked, "You're right, Sam, this is sure a tough course."

Everyone laughed, and they started off in great good humor. Unfortunately the man's mood changed. He went from bad to worse, getting more annoyed with himself at each hole. There was every reason for his annoyance. He missed easy putts, topped his drives, and sprayed shots left and right like a mowing machine. It took patience to work with him, and Robin walked endless miles through the rough looking for his balls. Once or twice he was slow in handing over the right club.

"C'mon, boy! C'mon there with that five iron," he snapped.

Once, by mistake, Robin gave him the wrong wood. "What's the matter, son? You aren't on the ball today!"

By the time they reached the fourteenth hole, Robin was exhausted. The sun beat down, the course was hard and baked, the bag was heavy. Everyone was weary and wet with sweat. Forgetting himself, he sank down on the grass near the tee while his player drove off. The drive hooked off again into the rough.

Turning, furious with himself, the man saw Robin sitting on the turf beside the tee, the bag between his knees. Instantly he exploded. "Confound it! Hang it all, boy! What the devil d'you mean, sitting down there when I'm driving? Don't you know how to caddie? You're supposed to be up watching my ball. You're paid to stay on the job. You've been slack and inattentive all afternoon. I'm just about tired of you. Go back to the caddie master, hear? Go back and tell him to send me out a boy who knows his stuff, who keeps his eye on my ball. Get moving. Drop that bag here."

Robin jumped. He laid the bag on the bench beside the tee and turned for the long walk back to the clubhouse, more tired than he had ever been in a track meet at school. This, he thought, must be how a pitcher feels when he is taken out of the game after the home-run hitters have been on him; this is the way a man suffers when he drops an easy fly in the last few minutes of the ninth inning.

The caddie master looked up as he entered the golf shop. Like everyone else, he was hot and tired after the long week end. "You finished, Bob?"

"No, sir, I was sent back."

"You were sent *back?* What for?"

"For sitting down at the fourteenth. He told me to come back and say for you to send out a boy who knows his stuff."

The caddie master fairly leaped from behind the counter. He whirled around to the door and shouted, "Hey there, Dave! Snap into it, quick. Get out to the sixteenth and grab Mr. Randall's bag. For Pete's sake, hurry, will ya?" Then he turned on Robin, more quietly but still upset and exasperated. "See here, son, this won't do! You're paid to work, to attend to business, not to sit on your tail out there. Know who that was? That was Mr. Randall, chairman of the greens committee. I'd rather have this happen to anyone in the club but him. He pays for service and he expects it, has a right to expect it, too. No wonder he got mad and chewed you up. You'll lose your fee and your tips for this round, and if it happens again you're through. I can't hold my job when the caddies do things of this sort. You play golf, don't you, fella? Sure you do. Well, you should know better'n that. You aren't a kid like some of these boys around here. Understand me?"

Robin nodded miserably. There wasn't a thing he could say, so he turned and went outside to the bench and slumped down. The boys around were jubilantly counting their cash and coming in to be paid off, shouting and yelling, roughhousing with each other. Their noisy, boisterous tones bothered Robin. He felt they were a gang of hooligans and he disliked them all. By rights he ought to be out beside the swimming pool with the Joans and Camillas and Penelopes, the girls he was used to playing with at Sweet Briar all summer.

Was it, he wondered, really worth it, this punishment? Was this seeing the world worth while? He pulled out of his pocket a letter he had received that morning from his mother but had hardly read. She was so delighted because he had split with Butch Morrison and was staying with the Haskells that she never even asked whether he had enough money.

He read the letter through, wiped his forehead, and rose to get a drink from the big coke cooler. The letter fell to the ground unnoticed. As he moved away, one of the younger caddies stepped over, picked it up, and glanced at it. The letter began as most mothers' letters do. "My darling Robin."

The boy who picked it up was a freckle-faced youngster of eleven who spent much of his time playing tricks on the other boys around the caddie house.

He seized the letter and waved it in his hand. "Hey, look, fellas, look!" Then in a high-pitched voice he shouted, "Oh, Robin. Robin darleeng . . ."

Robin turned, glaring. Instantly he saw his mother's letter held aloft in that grimy fist. This was the payoff, this at the end of the long, hot, unpleasant day. Had the boy been anywhere near his own age, he would have slugged him. Slowly he advanced, anger in his eyes, while the crowd watched openmouthed.

"Here! Gimme that letter!"

The boy hesitated. Then, seeing the look on Robin's face, he dropped the letter and scampered around to the other side of the clubhouse, where he was well out of reach. Silence fell over the tired, perspiring youngsters fingering their dollar bills. They watched Robin closely as he stood motionless. Then the youngster poked his face around the corner. "Oh, Robin," he called. "Oh, Robin! Robin darleeng . . ."

Chapter 7

ROBIN stepped up to the first tee. He leaned over, pegged up his ball, then turned to take a couple of practice swings. As he stood wiggling the driver, a high-pitched voice from somewhere behind a tree shrieked, "Oh, Robin! Oh, Robin darleeng . . ."

Snickers rose from the little group of caddies beside the tee. Robin gripped his club fiercely, scowled down the fairway, looked at the ball, and swung. He topped the ball and sent it rolling harmlessly for twenty yards. The snickering behind him became audible titters. As he bent over to pick up his tee, the infernal little brat resumed the attack. "Oh, Robin! Oh, you Robin!"

Monday was caddies' day at the club. The pool, the clubhouse, and the course were all open to the boys. That morning the pro was away and the caddie master was conducting the regular monthly tournament for the caddies. They had all been practicing and everyone was entered. It was this which had brought Robin back that morning. For, in addition to the prizes, the winner was to be allowed to caddie for Sammy Gorman, the Open Champion, who was coming to play an exhibition match that next Sunday, the Fourth of July.

The night before, Robin had wanted never to see Skokie again. His one desire was to get moving, to say good-by to the Haskells and head westward, to put as many miles as possible behind him. But the chance to play the course and possibly caddie for Sam Gorman conquered his reluctance to come back. So he showed up as usual.

On the first two holes everything went wrong that possibly could go wrong. He made mistakes that would have made him want to smile if he had been caddying for somebody else. He overdrove the short second; two iron shots caught the traps; an easy putt bounced out of the cup; and both times he faced the ball on the tee, his freckle-faced tormentor could be heard mocking him at a safe distance. "Oh, Robin! Oh, Robin darleeng . . ."

His instinct and training as a competitor told him to hold on. Somehow, he held on, kept his temper, and by the fourth hole was actually enjoying himself, liking the feeling of holding his own under pressure. This was a feeling he well knew—a feeling you get when the bar goes from ten-six to eleven, then to eleven-six and twelve; when the other man clears it easily each time. Somehow you must too.

Golf is a game demanding courage like most

games. But unlike other games, it needs a peculiar kind of concentration, the ability to control every reaction, to concentrate to the exclusion of everything else. This was a quality his vaulting practice had given him. He shook off his tormentor and began to seal himself into his game.

As his confidence returned, his touch came back too. On the fifth he sank his first long putt from the edge of the green. When he stepped to the sixth tee, the boy's voice could be heard as usual: "Oh, Robin! Oh, Robin darleeng . . ."

Suddenly other voices broke in. "Tha's enough, Stacey." "Beat it, Stacey." "Shut up, Stacey, he's driving. Now quit that," said the others in his foursome.

Robin had a birdie on that hole and, glancing up, noticed Stacey trailing slowly off over the rise of the fairway in the distance. He felt as if he had at least won one battle, even if he hadn't won the war.

On the seventh he might have been upset had he not been master of himself. Monday was caddies' day at the club, to be sure; yet you couldn't exactly keep members off their own course, even on a Monday. As a rule, however, few showed up that day. Robin recalled going round with Butch Morrison on caddies' day back at Sweet Briar, never noticing whether other members were playing or not. Here he saw things from a different angle.

Now he found he resented the two old gaffers who

were holding them up by looking for lost balls in the rough. On the next hole the boys were allowed to go through, and he walked over to the tee with his partners, each carrying his own bag.

Two of the younger members of the club were just driving off. They turned and surveyed the four caddies impersonally. Then the two players came back to the bench for their bags. One turned toward Robin. It was Tony Briggs.

Tony stepped over near him to pick up his bag, which was leaning against the bench. He glanced at Robin, looked straight at him, and never saw him. Tossing his bag on his shoulder, he turned and tramped off down the fairway, while Robin stood open-mouthed on the tee, watching him disappear in the distance.

Tony was one of the best pole vaulters in Eastern school circles, a rival Robin had met—and invariably defeated—at track meets indoors and out for several years. He was going to Harvard that fall. They were friends. They always shook hands cordially when they faced each other in track suits and spiked shoes. Yet here at Skokie, he didn't exist for Tony. It was not that Tony cut him; it was simply that because he was a caddie Tony did not even see him. He was a member and Robin was not.

Naturally he sliced his drive from the tee, but he quickly recovered with a beautiful second, and his third shot bounced right in front of the green. Then he forgot Tony and went from strength to strength. At the twelfth the boys were muttering behind him, comparing cards. At the fourteenth he overheard someone suggest he had a chance to beat Mac.

Mac was the oldest caddie and the best player. He was on the Northwestern golf team as a sophomore; when you spoke of Mac and his game, you did so with respect. Mac had never been beaten by any of them, yet here he was in danger from a boy out of the East with a strange way of talking and the queer name of Robin! No wonder the boys looked at each other as he continued to smack the ball, straight and far down the fairways.

He bore down on the fifteenth, got a par on each of the next two. Now the caddies began to advise him on his shots, to cluster around when he drove from the tee. On the seventeenth he smacked a beautiful iron shot onto the green in one, and from the last tee he noticed a small crowd up ahead. Theirs was the last foursome of the day. Someone must have notified Mac he was in danger.

A boy panted down from the clubhouse. "Hey, there, Bob, you have a chance to beat Mac. Ya know that? You have a good chance. You only need a five to do it."

He smiled, nodded, turned, and addressed the ball. Nobody moved, no one spoke, no raucous high-pitched voice jeered from behind a tree. There was a respectful silence as he drew his club back and swung.

Zzzzoooom . . . The ball sailed straight and low two hundred and fifty yards out on the grass.

"Zowie! He sure smacked that one," said a voice. "You're next, Jerry."

They tramped off the tee, and as they did so somebody grabbed Robin's bag. "No, no, lemme take it. You got a chance to beat Mac. You'll need a two or a three iron here against this wind."

They were no longer interested in their own scores; they wanted to see whether this boy with the sissy name could beat Mac. "Say, if you beat Mac on this course you're good! You really got it!"

Robin's third floated and fluttered between the traps and died gracefully on the apron of the green. A chorus of approval rose about him. Now he felt safe, for he had two putts to go down.

Steady now, he thought, steady does it. He struck the ball firmly, his head kept well down until he heard a ripple of hand clapping beyond the green. The ball was rolling gently straight for the pin. It died inches away. One more stroke, and he had won the caddie tournament and the right to carry Sam Gorman's bags next Sunday. The others crowded around, shaking his hand, congratulating him. Mac pushed through, his hand stuck out.

"Good going, Bob! Good work, fella. You can really powder that ball, you really can!"

Chapter 8

ROBIN stood just beyond a traffic light on Route 30 on the outskirts of Aurora, Illinois. In his pocket was a letter from Mr. Haskell to old Yale friends in Denver, and he was seventy-six dollars richer than when he arrived in Evanston. Such luck, he felt uneasily, was too good to last.

A caddie at Skokie, who had done lots of hitch-hiking through the Middle West, had advised him to take a bus out Roosevelt Road to the end of the highway at Aurora, a few miles from Chicago, and stand just beyond a traffic light. "Be sure and smile," the boy had said emphatically. "That helps a lot."

Smiling, Robin soon discovered, is hard work. At the end of the first fifteen minutes his jaws ached. He smiled and smiled and much good it did him. Whoosh . . . whoosh . . . whoosh went the Fords and Frazers, the Chevvies and Pontiacs.

After half an hour his face felt stiff. This, he felt, was in a way his first real test. The ride with the pieman was luck, and the break with Mr. Haskell would never happen again in a thousand miles. So

he stood patiently beyond the traffic light, grinning
while the cars whooshed past. Never before had he
tried to smile for twenty minutes on end. This was
no fun. Before long the smile became forced and
mechanical, and after a while it was a silly grin.

Robin knew the obvious things about getting a
lift. You must look clean. To be a student helps, so
he wore his white track sweater with the *T* inside
out. He recalled that you had to go to the outskirts
of town and stand just beyond a traffic light, where
cars would be moving slowly and could stop with
no difficulty.

Whoosh went the line of cars. Whoosh . . .
whoosh . . . whoosh! Gathering speed, they disappeared into the distance, leaving him there with
that foolish grin on his face.

Perhaps he had too much baggage. Of course, had
he contemplated hitching when he left home, he
would never have brought along his golf clubs or
that heavy suitcase, either. Everyone warned him
it wouldn't work with a bag of clubs, that drivers
never stop for hitchhikers with too much stuff. One
neat suitcase, yes; that shows you're not a tramp.
But a great heavy suitcase and a leather golf bag,
never.

Then an idea came to him. It had worked once;
it might work again. He unzipped his bag and
yanked out his number four wood. Turning his
back on the road, he swung casually a few times. He

waited, hoping to hear the sound of grinding brakes. Nothing could be heard but that eternal whoosh . . . whoosh . . . whoosh, as the cars rolled endlessly past.

This was no good. He might be here all day at this rate. He turned to one side and carelessly swung his club at an offensive weed. Then he returned to the side of the road and started to stuff the club back into the bag. As he did so, the welcome sound of brakes came to his ears. A blue Chevrolet was stopping up ahead. Robin lost no time. He grabbed his suitcase and golf bag, dropped the club to the ground in his confusion, picked it up, and finally reached the car. He shoved the two bags in the back, and sank panting on the front seat beside the driver.

"Thanks . . . Mister . . . thanks . . ."

He took a quick look at his companion. The man at the wheel was gray-haired, wore steel spectacles, and had a gray hat pulled down over his eyes. The back seat was filled with samples of some kind, so Robin guessed that he was a salesman.

"Where you going, son, the Tri-Cities?"

American geography, he was discovering the farther west he went, was not a subject really stressed at school. He had never heard of the Tri-Cities. All he knew was that they must lie westward, because the car was headed that way. He wanted to go in that direction, so he nodded.

"O.K. I live in East Moline. You can pick up a bus there to take you to town. Where you from?"

"Connecticut."

"Connecticut! My, you're a long ways from home, aren't you? Well, I don't usually pick up hitchhikers, but seeing you out there with those clubs, I figured . . ."

"Yes, sir. You a golfer too?"

Was he a golfer! He was indeed! "You bet! I play the Arsenal at Rock Island. Guess I've played almost every course in the state one time or another. Now you take that Des Moines Country Club, there . . ."

U.S. 30 was flat, straight, endless, and as different as possible from the winding, hilly roads at home. Vast fields of growing corn could be seen on both sides—new country for Robin. He was amazed at the size of the fields, the bigness of the farms, so unlike the small dairy farms back home. He wanted to ask questions, to find out about the farmers and farming, but as they moved toward the setting sun he had little chance. The man went on talking without interruption, giving detailed accounts of various clubs and various matches.

"So he called and said, 'Let's play this foursome at noon.' I get to the club about a quarter to twelve. Not a soul there but the pro, no one in the lockers, either. Around noon, well maybe a little after, my partner . . ."

From his hip pocket Robin sneaked a road map. He soon found the Tri-Cities—Rock Island, Davenport, and Moline, where the driver lived. It was a shock to discover how short a distance on the map they would have covered by nightfall. Although this was all new and strange enough to make him feel he was getting into the West, one glance at the map showed that he had a long way to go before the real West even began. Robin's heart sank; doubt sneaked into his mind. Could he make it, this long and uncertain journey? The United States, he realized, is a big land.

Meanwhile, the man at the wheel entertained him with a play-by-play description of his game, his scores, his partners, his winning bets, his best shots, and an endless account of how once he almost made a hole in one. Robin endeavored to listen. He discovered he had only to toss in an occasional question, and the man at the wheel would continue talking for miles without stopping. Actually, he showed little interest in anything except golf and none whatever in his young passenger until, toward the end of the trip he paused to draw breath and Robin remarked, "I caddied for Sammy Gorman."

The car wavered perceptibly on the road. For a moment the driver was stunned into silence. "No! When? Where?"

"Yesterday, at Skokie. He was giving an exhibition with Sandy Ferguson, the pro there."

"Well, well, Sammy Gorman! Think of that! Why didn't you tell me? I've seen Sammy play when we had the Western at the Tri-Cities. Tell me, what kind of a fellow is he?"

"Swell. He gave me ten bucks."

"No . . . no . . . I mean as a person, when you get close up to him."

"Oh, he's a grand guy. Much easier to work with than some of the members." Robin was thinking of Mr. Randall.

"H'm . . . h'm . . . yes, I suppose so. You caddie quite a lot, do you?"

"Yessir, I'm hitching across the country caddying. It's a way of getting there. See now, at most places you get a buck an hour and three dollars a round. With your tips you can average fifty a week. . . ."

But the man was far more interested in Sammy Gorman. "Tell me more about Gorman. What impressed you about his game? Did you learn anything?"

Robin thought. There was that wonderful approach over the water, dead to the pin, and the insolent ease with which he hooked his drive around a clump of trees on one hole. And then his chip shots, especially his chips . . .

"Yes, I believe I did learn something. 'Course, you know, this was an exhibition and all, but the thing that impressed me was that he never hurried. Never, on any shot. I've been walking up to the ball, looking at the hole, looking at the ball, and then . . . bang! That's no good."

"Most players do; most of us do," agreed the man. "Or else they stand there and wiggle their club all night."

"That's just it. Not Sammy Gorman, though. He seemed to be thinking over every shot before he hit it, and he took just as much time over a two-foot putt as over a twenty-foot one. He didn't walk up and stab at it, the way I do."

"Yes, I know exactly what you mean. I noticed that about him too. Well, well, so you caddied for Gorman. You're getting a lot of experience on this trip, aren't you? Now, son, if you want a caddie job in the Tri-Cities, I don't hardly advise you to try my club. It's a pretty flat course, all in all, and the members have caddie carts. You go to the Davenport course; that's a billy-goat course where they usually need boys. You'll pick up a job there, all right. Tell the pro Harry Stevens of the Arsenal Club sent you over."

The man dropped Robin at a street corner near the outskirts of town, where he turned off for his home. At one point he had offered to run Robin downtown, but since Robin had no idea where he was going he insisted on getting off at the corner. There, so his friend said, a bus would take him into the city. They shook hands. Robin retrieved his two bags from the rear of the car and stepped out.

The bus was a long while coming. Robin was hungry, having eaten nothing since early morning, and grew impatient. It was after six, most of the traffic was moving in the opposite direction, and the few cars going toward town were traveling fast. However, he felt he might as well try for a ride, so he stood well out in the gutter and held up his right arm. Almost immediately a car stopped, pulled back. It was a prowl car and a policeman stepped out. He was an enormous man with a vast stomach. A leather belt was wrapped around his middle, and a revolver hung from his hip.

Now what? Robin wondered.

"Where you from, young fella? Lemme see your papers." Robin fumbled in his pocket as the cop went on. "You a deserter?"

He was shocked. "Deserter?" he repeated. The idea had hardly occurred to him that sometimes men do desert from the armed forces. "Deserter! Why, no! I'm under age."

The cop instantly took another line. "Oh, you running away from home, are ya?"

"No, sir. My folks know I'm on the road. I have a letter here from my mother." He fumbled furiously for his wallet.

"What's your name, son?"

"Robert B. Longe." At last he had his purse, opened it, and found his driver's license.

"That your real name?" The cop glared at him.

"Why, sure. Of course it's my real name."

The officer extended a huge paw and took the license. This was something new to Robin. Why on earth shouldn't he give his real name? Then he remembered Mr. Haskell's letter written on the business stationery of his firm. He pulled the envelope from his pocket and yanked out the note. "Here. This man's a great friend of my father's. He lives in Evanston."

The cop read the letter, folded it up, and handed it back. "I guess you're all right. Only watch yourself, son."

To his amazement, Robin found himself shaken by this, his first encounter with the law. There was no reason whatever to be nervous; there was nothing to worry about. But he disliked standing there in the gutter as cars whizzed past and people looked curiously at the two of them.

"Where you going, young fella, the downtown Y.?" the cop asked, not without kindness in his tone.

Actually, Robin hadn't the slightest idea where he was going, but the Y. seemed as good a place as any. Some boys, he knew, slept in a railroad station or a bus terminal, and he might have to before long. But now he had some money, so he nodded. The cop turned and held open the trunk of the car, and Robin jumped to his baggage. It was Robin's first ride in a police car and he was interested in it.

"O.K., son, just watch your step. Lots of hitchhikers get themselves in trouble these days, so you better look out. I see you're a golfer. Play a lot?"

"Yes, sir, are you a golfer too?" He thought this the tactful thing to say, although a cop with a large stomach hardly seemed the type to be an athlete.

"Yep, I play the Muni course on my day off. I usta shoot a pretty fair game, too. Few years ago I was in the low eighties. We had the Western Open out here a couple of years ago. I saw Sammy Gorman and all the big shots. Quite an experience."

He continued as they sped rapidly through downtown traffic. Drivers pulled away from the curb without warning, exceeded the speed limit, shot through stop signs without pausing. But the fat cop was far too busy, telling about the time he had played a match for the city title twenty years before and lost on the eighteenth hole, to notice anything. It was a long story, and he finished every detail before he let Robin alight at the Y.

It was beginning to look as if everybody in the United States played or had played the game of golf.

Chapter 9

G UESS I'll have to walk a way, bags and all, Robin thought. It would be better than being stuck in this spot, a million miles from any place. With night coming on, too.

The spot was a lonely crossroads about twenty miles east of Iowa City, where a friendly farmer had dropped him after a discouraging day with long waits in a torrid sun and few rides. Robin had been glad to get out of the car, because the man roared along at seventy-five an hour, one hand on the wheel, the other out of the car window and resting on the roof.

But, alone beside the road, he almost longed now for that speeding farmer. This was a dismal place. Nothing save cornfields could be seen in any direction, no houses, no barns, no lights, nothing. A traffic signal at the crossroads would have slowed the cars down; but, as it was, they rushed past at frightful speeds. Worst of all was the approaching dusk. This was the first time he had been caught out at dusk, and he resolved it would be the last.

Let's see, this is Thursday. He glanced at his watch. Eight-thirty. That peaceful period after dinner when the whole family sat together a few minutes on the porch, when Dad asked the usual question about his practice, when most likely the telephone would ring, and his mother, being nearest, would answer. Then she would call to him, "It's a young lady, Robin, a young lady for you. She didn't give me her name." There would be a strong note of disapproval in her voice.

Then he remembered her last letter, received that morning at the post office before leaving the Tri-Cities. He pulled it from his pocket. Her small handwriting was just visible in the dying light.

Darling Robin,

Your grand letter telling us about Gorman and the exhibition match arrived this morning, and both Dad and I enjoyed it so much. Dad said you described him very well in a few words. I can see you are having great experiences, and I'm happy for you. And you have really been good about writing.

The heat here has been terrible. Yesterday the office was closed at noon. The Sound has been glassy, and of course no sailing, though I expect the heat out your way is worse, for we do usually manage a breeze off the water at night. We follow your progress west and rejoice at the way you are getting on so well by yourself. No doubt you'll have many setbacks and discouragements ahead, but you'll overcome them, I'm sure. Always remember, if things get unbearable, you can come back any time and we'll welcome you with open arms.

Tears came to his eyes. Hang it, that's idiotic! You don't cry when you're grown up, almost ready for college. It's absurd. But somehow I don't believe I ever felt so lonesome before.

Automobile lights flashed endlessly past. He could see them far, far down the road and watch them coming closer. It was nineteen miles to the nearest town, and he realized nobody was going to pick him up there in the dark. So it was walk or nothing.

He slung his golf bag over his shoulder, lifted his suitcase, crossed the highway in order to face the oncoming lights, and started off. Five minutes convinced him that walking was impossible. Heavy thundershowers had soaked the ground, making it a soggy marsh on both sides of the road. Unless somebody stopped, he was due for his first night under the stars.

The thought worried him as he trudged doggedly on, ducking aside when lights showed up, walking on the road when there were no cars coming. His bags were heavy and the heat bore down on him. Out here the heat persisted after dark. Finally he reached a small bridge where the highway passed over a stream. He could go no farther and the bridge, he thought, might provide shelter if it rained again. He climbed down the bank and, sure enough, the ground under one end of the bridge was dry and solid. He dumped down his bags, took off his shoes, rolled up his coat for a pillow, and stretched out in relief.

Half past nine, his watch said. I've got eight or nine hours of this before the cars start moving again. He soon found, however, that, tired as he was, sleep on that hard ground was impossible. I'm scared, he thought. I don't like this. I'm not used to the strangeness of it all, to the blackness all about, to being here alone. Well, I wanted to be on my own; I sure am now.

This is the first time I've ever been afraid, he reflected. Always in tight places, in track meets and tournaments, I've been top dog. I felt sure of winning, so naturally I never got worried, never had stage fright. This is different! In this darkness things seem to be moving all the time. It's terrible to be alone with all these strange noises around. Butch would think it was fun. I kinda wish Butch was here now. . . .

Thoughts of all kinds assailed him, stirred by his imagination or his memory. He recalled stories of boys robbed and thrown from moving cars for their money. He had read about one who was knocked over the head and left by the roadside merely for a wrist watch. Maybe those stories were true. Wait a minute. . . . There! Was that something or someone over there? He peered into the darkness, afraid to move, yet even more afraid to sit still. Look, I might as well go over and see what it is as die of fright here. So, taking a short number seven iron noiselessly from his bag, he crept over and poked around.

Nothing . . . space . . . nothing. The space under the bridge was empty. It only made him feel more lonely.

Then he remembered the last sentence in his mother's letter. Hadn't he really had enough? He had reached the Middle West on his own. What was the sense of going ahead? Why not quit? Was it really smart to take this punishment when there was no obligation to do so? What did it all prove, anyhow? He could spend the rest of the summer sailing with Pamela on the Sound. Her father had a sweet little thirty-two-footer he could handle perfectly. Or he could be out on the fairways at Sweet Briar every afternoon. And he could sleep in a clean, comfortable bed, not on a hard piece of ground that made his bones ache. It was tempting and so easy, too.

All he had to do was get back to the Haskells' and put in a collect call for his father. Airplane fare to New York would be in his hands within a few hours. He needn't really go back to Evanston, either. At the next town, at the next pay station, he could drop in a coin and hear Dad's voice, cool, resourceful, surprised at nothing.

"Well, Robin old boy, how are you? Coming back? Good, good! We certainly will be glad to see you. Why, yes, certainly. I'll call my secretary in New York and have her wire you a hundred and fifty by Western Union right away. What's the name of the town there?"

Yes, it would be simple. No more taking orders from peppery old hackers on a golf course. No more twisting his face into a smile until it ached. And no more staying out under a lonely sky at night, no more discomfort, and mosquitoes biting you every minute, and . . .

Dad was not the sort who would say, "I told you so." He would just accept things, listen with interest to Robin's experiences, and ask him if he didn't want to go down and take a swim before dinner.

No, I guess not. I guess I'd better not give in. I started out to do something and I better not quit. If I went home now I'd be a pole vaulter and end up at Yale. Pole vaulting and Yale! But would that be so awful, he wondered . . . he wondered. . . .

Something thundered overhead. It was a truck passing over the bridge. Robin glanced up, startled and dazed. Why, it's light; it's morning now. I must have slept. Somehow I fell asleep. He grabbed for his suitcase and his golf bag. Both were at his side, intact. Phew! That's lucky! Anyone could have pinched them while I slept.

Wearily he went down to the muddy water of the

stream, pulled a comb out of his suitcase, wet his hair, and combed it. Then he dusted off his trousers as well as he could, took his bags, and climbed the slippery bank.

He looked at his watch. It was seven-thirty. Already the world was steaming, the air lifeless. Last night, he thought, I had a chocolate bar for dinner. The nearest town is miles away. Wonder if I could walk it carrying this load of junk. I'm really hungry now. If nobody gives me a lift, if I stand here very long without a ride, guess I really will chuck the whole thing. This punishment is grim.

A car came slowly toward him out of the sun. Robin saw it was a farm truck with high board sides, evidently carrying an animal of some sort in the rear. He held out his hand and managed a weary smile. The truck drew closer; the driver looked at him and came to a stop.

Chapter 10

GRADUALLY he became more adept at getting rides, and as he went along he began to learn to take the endless waits beside the road in his stride. With this came an assurance toward the different situations and the various people he met along the way.

"I'm only going as far as Des Moines." "That's just fine for me, sir."

"I'll haul ya as far as Grand Forks, Bud. How's that suit ya?" "Grand Forks is great. Thanks lots," replied Robin, not knowing whether Grand Forks was twenty miles ahead or a hundred.

"Council Bluffs O.K. for you, fella?" "You bet. Council Bluffs is right on my way. It's west of here, isn't it?" Wherever they were going, as long as the car was headed toward the setting sun, was right for Robin.

Slowly the cornfields of Iowa changed to the great square farms of Nebraska, farms larger than any he had ever seen or dreamed about, farms that sometimes took four or five minutes to drive past. He was fascinated by everything and everyone, by the friendliness of the people, by the way they called him by his first name and then an hour later introduced him as "my friend Bob, from Connecticut."

The farms were different from the New England farms he was used to, both in size and aspect. Instead of the neat white houses with the red barns, many were unpainted board and looked run down. Yet people seemed prosperous and the roads were full of Packards and Lincolns.

Another thing astonished Robin. People were fiercely loyal to their state in a way that amazed him. Iowa, he was told, has no state debt. It leads the country in the production of corn, possesses fifty-one institutions of higher learning, tops the nation with ninety-nine per cent literacy. He had never thought about Connecticut in the passionate way these people thought about their home state.

Every day he saw sights that were new and puzzling. Great machines off on the horizon working in echelon on the huge farms. Trailer camps well off the road in the middle of nowhere. He asked about one of them.

"Migratory workers," explained the driver he questioned. "Those folks live the year round in trailers, whole families of 'em. Kids go to school wherever they happen to be. They start work in the Panhandle down in Texas in the spring and come north gradually, getting clean up to the Canadian border."

"You mean they go from the south to the north every year?"

"That's right. They follow the season, work the crops as they go. They'll cover several thousand miles or more each year. Make big money, too. Why, there's Mexicans working for those people who own their own trailers. They cost five thousand dollars, too."

The United States, Robin realized again every day, is a big land.

He knew now that hitchhiking is a business, to be learned like any other business. He discovered also that as he got farther west, not everybody played golf. Swinging a golf club beside the highway still occasionally brought results, but more often only stares from the folks in the cars that went whoosh . . . whoosh . . . whoosh past him. Sometimes just leaning on a driver and smiling made folks stop, but usually the only method was patience. Patience brought results, but being patient under the burning sun of midsummer was far from easy.

He soon discovered salesmen were his best bet. In those days after leaving the Tri-Cities, he met salesmen of all kinds, old and young, salesmen for brushes and agricultural machinery, for hats and hosiery. They insisted on buying his meals and charging them to their expense accounts. At first this bothered Robin, for he was trying to earn his own trip, but the salesmen wouldn't hear of his spending his own money.

Gradually Robin got the knack of being an attentive listener, of looking with interest at the picture of the driver's wife and children, of asking the right questions about his business or his golf score, of pulling Pamela's picture out of his wallet at the correct moment. Slowly he became more and more interested in people, although he realized that after the shock of surprise at finding him so far from home they were much more interested in themselves and their own problems.

Slowly Robin became less clumsy in approaching people. Folks who did stop were usually kind, although he ran into some strange characters occasionally. One big man who overflowed the whole front seat eyed Robin suspiciously before he opened the car door. "You a college boy?" he demanded.

"Going to Yale next year," Robin was surprised to find himself saying.

"Well, you're a long ways from home, aren't you?" The man drove on, apparently relieved. "Yale, hey? That's a rich man's school."

Robin was surprised and annoyed. "It is *not*," he protested. "Half the men at Yale are there on scholarships."

"Oh," said the man apologetically. "Now I didn't know that."

More and more, as he got into the West, Robin found himself in the strange position of defending Yale, the same Yale he was so weary of at home. He reflected as they drove along that things looked very different in the middle of Iowa from the way they seemed in Five Mile River, Connecticut. Usually he refused to argue with strangers who insisted Yale was a country club full of millionaires' sons, and merely ended the discussion by remarking, "Well, I imagine there are worse places than Yale." There never seemed to be any answer to this.

There were more hitchhikers on the roads now: young fellows changing jobs, service men going home, college boys on vacation. Frequently along the highway he saw them standing with thumbs extended and large white signs at their feet: *U of C, 1955;* or *Idaho, 1956;* or *Stanford, 1955.* Once there was a soldier with a large pack at his side and a sign reading, "I'm tired of walking."

One morning, to Robin's amazement, a car drew up ahead and the woman driver leaned out, actually beckoning to him. He grabbed his luggage and ran forward. By the time he caught up with her, she had opened the rear door of the car. However, he soon understood her politeness. Wedged tight in the back seat with half a dozen pillows was a squalling child about two years old. Several small youngsters eyed him curiously from the front.

"Hold him," commanded the lady.

Robin obeyed. Dumping his suitcase and golf bag on the floor, he picked up the child. Well, I've been a lot of things since leaving Five Mile River, he thought, but this is the first time I've been a baby sitter. The child spit in his face, snatched at his hair, twisted, squirmed, and bawled for the next sixty miles. True, it was sixty miles nearer the Pacific, but Robin was not exactly sorry when the lady said that she was turning off for her farm and he could get out.

As he did so he saw an interesting figure beside the road. Tall, thin, blond, he was a boy about his own age, clad in a shirt and khaki shorts which exposed two bony knees. At one foot was an enormous pack, from his shoulder hung a camera, at his hip was a canteen, and in his limp left hand he held a British flag. His hair was disheveled, his face red from the heat; he was painfully hot, dusty, travel-stained. So was Robin. Yet as he stood there with his golf bag and suitcase he felt like a traveler de luxe.

The stranger eyed him. "Hello."

"Hello. My name's Bob Longe."

The stranger seemed embarrassed. He extended a hand. "Hugh Gathwick," he mumbled.

Here's something, Robin thought. I meet up with a Britisher on the Nebraska plains. It did not take long to discover that the stranger had landed in Manhattan a month before with no money, that he had done odd jobs all across the country and, thanks to that and the help of kindly people on the road, now had almost thirty-four dollars in his pocket-book. His story made Robin, who had been feeling like Leif Ericson, very humble.

"I'll hand it to you. You've really got it," he said, thinking it most unlikely that Dad would ever allow him to visit England with no cash. "Well, now you've seen a lot of this country, how d'you like it?"

"That's what everyone asks," answered the stranger, holding up his flag to a passing Packard, whose occupants all turned with astonishment as they whizzed by. "I think America is ripping, all except this heat. It was just a hundred at that town back there. But I'm doing what I wanted to do. I'm seeing the real Americans."

Robin was puzzled. "You mean the Indians?"

"Oh, no." He waved his flag tentatively. "I mean the ones who stay home, who never travel abroad. I wanted to meet them."

"Oh, I see. Have you?"

"Rather," said the boy, with enthusiasm. "Yes, indeed. Everyone has been frightfully kind."

They stood in the hot sun exchanging experiences. Robin discovered the stranger was a year older than himself, lived in a suburb of London, was about to go to Oxford the next term. His father was a solicitor—the same thing as a lawyer, he explained, in the United States. Everyone in England had told him he was crazy and that he would never be able to see the United States with less than five hundred dollars. "Actually, I'm glad I had no money. I rather think I've met more interesting people and seen more this way than if I had been rich. I did have five dollars when I started. A G.I. at Harrow gave it to me. He asked me to buy a beer for him in Dallas. Do we go near Dallas on this road?"

Robin laughed. "I should say not. Not within . . . oh, I guess a couple of thousand miles. Dallas is down in Texas. Well, from what you've seen, would you like to come back?"

"Indeed I should," answered the Britisher, waving his flag at a car whose occupants merely stared. "Indeed I should. This is the way, really, to see the United States."

He was fascinating and the conversation was interesting, but time passed and nobody stopped. It was getting late and Robin did not intend to spend another night beside the road. But the cars were all going east toward a small town about fifteen miles away. The few that scurried past traveling west went faster and faster into the dusk.

"D'you think we should separate?"

"Mightn't we go back?" suggested the Englishman.

"Back? Where to?"

"Back to that town called Homestead. You must have passed through it this afternoon. The cars are all going that way. If we crossed the road, perhaps someone would stop, someone going to town."

The idea of retracing their steps was not exactly profound, yet it had never occurred to Robin. Always, at any cost, he had kept pressing west. Now he realized this was a mistake that had caused him trouble, including that dismal night under the bridge. They crossed the road and within ten minutes a farmer, who was taking his family to a movie in a small truck, stopped to pick them up.

When the car stopped in the town, the two boys found themselves in the town square. A large courthouse, surrounded with grass and benches, was in the middle. Here again Robin got a lesson. Now he began to realize what cheap travel was.

To his amazement, the Britisher went up to a policeman and asked for the jail. It appeared the jail was in the courthouse. Lugging his suitcase and golf bag, feeling exceedingly foolish, Robin followed his friend. At the jail entrance Hugh asked for the sheriff. Together they clumped up the wooden stairs to the second floor.

The big man behind the desk with his hat on the back of his head eyed them suspiciously, and asked to see the Britisher's passport. "And you?" he asked, turning to Robin. "Where you from, son?"

"From Connecticut."

"Connecticut! Say, you kids are sure a long way from home. What d'you want?"

Robin had no idea what they wanted, but Hugh proved to be a persuasive talker and before long the sheriff had agreed to let them occupy a cell in the jail for the night. As they entered the hot, stifling cubbyhole, after being fingerprinted and duly entered, Robin was not sure he would enjoy the night. However, he had to admit it was a new and interesting experience.

Following a cheap and horrible meal, they turned in. Robin's bunk was too hard to sleep on and there was a rumpus at two A.M. when the town drunk was brought in and put to bed. All in all, this was not the most comfortable night of his trip, although he had to admit it was one of the cheapest.

The next morning the sheriff came round at seven sharp. After they had washed, he insisted on taking them to his home, where his wife produced an enormous breakfast of bacon and eggs and wheat cakes. Then the sheriff took them in his car to a crossroads about five miles out of town, and there he began to stop passing cars. When he discovered one that was going several hundred miles, he beckoned to the boys. "These kids are a coupla strangers, Mac. Now treat 'em right." He shook hands and wished them both good luck as they climbed into the back seat.

Robin was elated over his new friend and his experience the previous night. This would surely be something to tell Pamela Griswold, that he had slept one night in jail. But he realized he had better not mention it at home. Mothers are funny about these things.

He turned to the Britisher, who was furling up his little flag. "Well now, tell me, how would you describe this country?"

The stranger looked out of the window across the waving plains, flat and straight right up to the horizon. He appeared to hesitate, then uttered two words. "Vast, vast," he said.

It was not in the least what Robin expected; it was not at all the way he would have put it. Yet it was an excellent description of the United States in two words.

Chapter 11

IT was indeed strange to be learning about life in the United States from an Englishman. Yet, before they parted company, Hugh Gathwick taught Robin many things about his own land and how to get around it, especially how to travel with little or nothing to use for money. He learned, for one thing, that if you missed a meal or two it was annoying but no calamity. Moreover, it saved cash.

The scenery changed as the two journeyed westward. The plains gave way to exciting vistas of mountain ranges far in the distance. The names of the towns told their own story: Broken Bow, Indianola, Kit Carson, Elk Springs, Arapahoe, Rawhide, Bonanza. They were fascinating to Robin.

When they finally reached Denver, Robin's funds were getting low and he felt he ought to stop and earn some money. Hugh Gathwick was going on, so they said good-by after the Britisher promised to visit Five Mile River on his return east. Then Hugh took his travel-stained pack and his silk flag, and hopped a bus to the outskirts of town for a ride west.

Robin saw him go with an unhappy feeling. After several days of friendly and helpful companionship in the trials of the road, he didn't welcome being on his own again. But he had Mr. Haskell's letter to friends in Denver, where he hoped for some home cooking, a clean bed for a change, and a chance to save money and build up his fortunes.

The first thing he did was to stop at the general-delivery window at the post office. There were three fat letters from home awaiting him and, better still, a laundry box full of clean clothes. Inside was a fresh pair of flannel trousers, clean shirts and shorts, and a pair of sneakers. Now, he felt, he would not look like a tramp when he met Mr. Haskell's friends.

Yes, that's the right kind of mother to have, he thought, as he took Mr. Haskell's letter from his pocket, checked the name, and found the telephone number. He dialed it and a woman's voice responded.

No, the Bensons were not there. The woman, a caretaker, explained that they were in the Yellowstone for three weeks, the whole family. Who should she say called? Robin mumbled his name with a sinking heart. This, he knew, was the worst news he could have had. Now he was on his own in a strange city.

First he took a three-dollar room in a dingy hotel, managed a shower bath down the hall, changed his clothes, repacked the laundry box with his dirty things, and sent it home express collect. Then, rocked by the bad news, he took a bus to the country club, where he was rocked for the second time that morning. They had no need for caddies.

After a while he found Overland Park; no luck there, either. It was early afternoon when he reached the municipal course, and they also had more caddies than they needed. There were plenty of college boys at home now and they were glad to caddie.

Now Robin really was worried. After eating a cheap meal, he went looking for a job, any job. Everybody asked the same question: What can you do? No use saying, "I can handle a thirty-two-footer in a storm like nobody's business," or, "I can pole-vault twelve-six under pressure." He had no special trade and no special abilities and he soon discovered that he couldn't get a job.

Meanwhile, his money was melting away. In the afternoon he stumbled into an employment agency, where a woman behind the desk asked the same question. Then she suggested tentatively that perhaps at least he could wash dishes.

"Yes, I can," responded Robin eagerly. He felt he knew kitchen work. He had waited on table regularly at school, taking turns with the other boys, and once during an influenza epidemic, when the kitchen staff was mostly sick, he had been one of the boys who volunteered to help. Indeed he knew kitchens, he could wash dishes.

"Good," replied the woman. "Check in at Matt's Café on Broadway below Colefax. Here, I'll show you on a map. They need someone, so go right over."

It seemed a pleasant enough place as he walked through the restaurant. But from the kitchen, looking out, it was not exactly inspiring. In fact, it was as different from the gleaming kitchen at school as anything could be. The equipment was ancient, the floor grimy. The restaurant itself was air-conditioned, but the kitchen was smoky and stifling. It was small, crowded and, even to his uncritical eye, dirty. The proprietress handed him an apron and a dishcloth, and indicated mountains of dishes in a sink.

The dish-washing machines had broken down, so with the help of a Mexican girl of about fourteen he stood washing dishes in greasy water for the next six hours. Then he received his dinner and six dollars. Not for the first time that summer did he look back with longing on the food at school.

Robin had never before stood six hours working in one spot; he found it exhausting. Perhaps the conditions did not help, for the place was fly-infested, smelly, and extremely noisy. But there he remained, running a greasy mop over the wet dishes, shoving them under the faucet, stacking them in trays at one side, while the proprietress constantly urged him to hurry.

He decided that one more day there would be all he could stand. Early the next morning he checked out of his hotel, took his baggage to the bus station, where he left it, and went back to work at the restaurant. At ten o'clock that evening he wandered over to the city park. A band concert was in progress. This was free and lasted until almost eleven.

In order to save the three dollars for a room, he had planned to sit up in the bus station until morning; but the night was not cold, the stars shone, and since a few soldiers and several other men seemed to be preparing to spend the night in the park, he decided to stretch out on an empty bench. He lay there wondering how many people slept outdoors at night in the United States, realizing things he had never suspected before. It was uncomfortable, this business of learning, in many ways.

The blow stung the sole of his foot. Never in his life had he been hit like that before. He came out of a troubled doze, cramped, angry, confused, to find a bright light in his face. A rough voice addressed him. "What you doing here, fella?"

Robin sat up, blinking, rubbing his eyes. His foot stung badly. The light was still turned on him, but in a minute he could distinguish two men standing over him in threatening attitudes, one in an army uniform, the other a policeman.

"I . . . I was sleeping . . . trying to . . ."

"Yeah. We seen you. Where you from?"

"Connecticut." His foot burned. Wearily he reached in his hip pocket for his purse, his driver's license, his identification cards.

Denver, he thought! I hate Denver! Nothing worked out here. I wish to goodness I'd gone on with Hugh Gathwick and taken chances with what cash I had. Denver!

"Here." He handed over his driver's license. Yet still they kept the light full on his face, save when it was playing up and down his body while they inspected his clothes. It annoyed and upset him.

"You ever been in the army?"

"No, I'm sixteen. I'm not a deserter. I'm not running away from home. My name is Robert B. Longe."

"Fresh guy, huh," said the policeman. "Let's run this character in."

Robin sat up, wide awake now. Run me in! What for? I've done nothing! They can't do that, they can't pinch . . . What right have they got. . . .

The soldier replied carelessly, "Leave us look at his papers." He calmly took the purse from Robin's hand and opened it, fumbling through the cards and papers without ceremony. He discovered Pamela's photograph, turned it upside down, then right side up, studied it with care. Robin was angry, yet knew he must not show it.

"You got any money?" Together they emptied

the purse, counted his precious dollar bills, fingered his license.

"Where d'you say you was from?"

"Like it says there—Five Mile River, Connecticut." Hugh Gathwick had discovered this trick and warned him. Cops asked you the same question several times to catch you up if possible.

"What you say your name was?"

"Robert B. Longe," he replied. It was easy to see they were trying to trip him if they could. He was still blinking, for the light was blinding him. He wished they would at least stop flashing the light in his eyes. But they held it on him steadily.

"Why don't we hold him twenty-four hours and see if there's any charges against him? You sure you never been in the army?"

"Yep, I'm sure, I'm sixteen. I was in school in Connecticut till June. I'm hitching west. There's my Amateur Athletic Union card there. . . ." He was worried now, because one night in jail had been quite enough.

"We better take him along and play it safe," insisted the cop.

"Aw, forget it," replied the soldier, still admiring Pamela's photograph. He stuck it in the purse and handed it back. "Only you can't sleep here in the park, Mac. You can sit here, sure, but if you sleep we'll lock you up next time. We'll pick you up on our next round. Understand?"

Robin nodded. He found himself trembling all over and hoped they hadn't noticed. At last the light left his face and he was in complete darkness. The two men moved down the row of benches, flashing the light, questioning someone else. With relief he watched them go over at last to a prowl car by the curb and drive slowly away.

Well, that's something. You can sit in the park all night, but you can't stretch out and be comfortable.

A soldier came toward him. "Forget them guys," he advised. "They only get here once a night. I know. I've been sleeping here for a week."

Robin thanked him but decided on the bus station, where at least nobody would smack the sole of his shoe. His foot stung as it touched the ground. "Ouch! That hurts!"

Denver! I hate Denver! I wish I'd never seen the place. If anyone tells me how beautiful Denver is, I'll give 'em an earful.

All morning he wavered between chucking the whole thing and giving it one more try. He stood waiting an eternity at a traffic light on the outskirts of the city on the main highway west, wondering whether it really was worth while.

Standing in the hot sun, his arm extended as the cars whizzed by, he remembered some of the pleasant things he was missing. Most of all he thought about his comfortable bed in his room at home overlooking the Sound. After that night in the park and the bus station, that bed seemed more attractive than ever. Almost he hoped nobody would stop, that he would be forced to return to town and send his father a wire.

Several hours later those thoughts vanished. He was riding with a friendly rancher from the other side of the range. Up they went, up, up, up along the slopes of the mountain ahead, up a curving, twisting road. They drove for some time with the snowy peaks beyond glittering in the sun. Robin grew really excited. Never had he realized mountains could be so thrilling. At one place they came to a sign by the roadside: *Loveland Pass, 11,992 feet.*

Almost twelve thousand feet, higher than he had ever been before! This was truly a thing to write home about. This alone, this sight of the great mountains towering above and around, this was worth everything. As they circled the pass, descended a little, and went through another gap in the mountains, the rancher explained the meaning of the words Robin had kept hearing: the Great Divide.

"It's the dividing line of the continental watershed. You see, son, this range stretches clean from the Canadian border down almost to Mexico. On one side the waters flow east and south. On the western side the rivers flow west and south. That's why they call it the Continental Divide."

Now every minute was exciting. Watching the

great summits change color as the sun rose higher
and higher, seeing the road twisting below among
the passes, Robin was happy because his sleepless
night, his discouragement in Denver, had not made
him give up.

At Glenwood Springs, down in the valley, the
rancher dropped him. After a while Robin decided
to get a sandwich at a small restaurant across the
street. The man at the counter beside him turned
out to be going west and, after a short conversation,
offered to take him along. This was an unexpected
break, which he eagerly accepted, soon finding himself shooting westward again at seventy an hour.

The driver was sent out by a concern making
roadside diners, and at first he proved interesting.
He rattled off facts and figures and general information about the roadside diners that were fascinating.
"How long? Eighty feet long, sixteen high." "Equipment? Sure it comes equipped, completely. Has a
stove, refrigerator, sink, dishwasher, plumbing,
everything."

But as the sun sank lower and penetrated the car,
the air became hotter and the man's endless information became less interesting. Robin was tired after a
sleepless night. He couldn't think of any more sensible questions to ask, so he let the man chatter on
about profit and loss, owners who made fortunes in
diners and retired to California, and so forth.

Toward the end of the long afternoon Robin

found it difficult to stay awake. He dozed. Suddenly he was brought up sharply by a poke in the ribs and a grim laugh.

"Hey there, fella, I picked you up to talk to me. Now, dammit, talk!"

Robin pulled himself together and sleepily asked a question. Immediately the man replied, and at once launched into a monologue that lasted for eighteen miles.

At Grand Junction they were nearing the Utah line. The man dropped him in the center of town and went off with a customer, first advising Robin to try a diner at the western end of the small town.

"A lot of truckers eat there," he said. "If you can grab yourself a trucking job, you've got a long haul ahead, son. Those fellas really travel. Good luck to you."

Chapter 12

ROBIN walked out to the diner and decided to eat some dinner before trying for a ride west. If he had no luck, he could return to town and get in at a tourist home for the night. The diner proved to be full of tired drivers, most of whom wore blue jeans, blue jumpers, and caps over their eyes. Robin noticed that many were warmly dressed.

"Franks and beans," they sang out, as they came in and took stools at the counter. Accordingly, Robin ordered the same thing, with a glass of milk. He eyed the apple pie longingly, decided it was two days old, and held off. He ate his meal and drank the milk, wondering what the resourceful Hugh Gathwick would do in such a situation. For although men on both sides talked to him and nodded when he explained he was hiking west, nobody offered a ride. Finally he rose, paid his check to the fat lady behind the cash register, and stood hopefully waiting at the door.

"Not going west, are you, Chief?" "Not going west, are you, Cap?"

He asked man after man as they paid their checks and went out. Each one looked at him queerly, said nothing, passed on. He felt sure it was his baggage—too much stuff. Not for the first time he wished he was traveling like the Englishman, with nothing but a pack slung on his back.

When he had just about decided things were hopeless, the woman behind the cash register leaned over and whispered, "You hiking to the Coast, son?"

He nodded eagerly. "Yes'm, I am."

"Why don't you wait just outside then? You'll have better luck out there. These men aren't supposed to pick up hitchers, and they don't dare take chances in here because someone might see them. Step out and speak to them when they leave."

"Gee, thanks! Thanks lots." Picking up his bag and his suitcase, he went out, placing himself beside the entrance. Before long a young fellow in gray trousers, gray shirt, gray cap on the back of his head, chewing a toothpick, stepped out. He looked at Robin, saw the golf bag, and said, "Watcha got there, Mac, golf clubs?"

"Yes, sir."

"Leave me heft one. I b'lieve I haven't swung a driver in two years." He reached in with a practiced hand, yanked out a driver, and, stepping to one side, swung the club with an easy, fluent motion. "Now that sure feels good! I'd like to go out and shoot some golf this minute." He stood taking beautiful swings while Robin prayed he was headed toward the setting sun with his truck.

"You couldn't give me a lift west, could you?"

Two truckers in pea jackets came down the steps. "Hi, Scotty." "Hi there, Scotty-boy."

"Why, hello, fellas, hello. Not a chance, Mac. I'm sorry, it's against the rules. Y'see that sign there on the side—no riders?" He replaced the driver, as Robin's disappointment grew, for he seemed an amusing chap. "You mean to say," his voice lowered, "you mean to tell me you going all the way to the Coast with that-there bag of clubs?"

"Yes, sir! All the way from Connecticut, too." He tried to keep the note of pride out of his voice.

"No kidding! Hitching with a bag of golf clubs! All the way from the East!" His admiration was plain enough. "Well, good for you, Mac, that's really something!"

Several truckers, hats on the back of their heads and toothpicks in their mouths, descended the steps, and he nodded casually. "Nope, no riders, son. Strictly against company rules," he repeated loudly, as the men moved out to the line of trucks along the highway.

"Of course, now . . ." His voice dropped again. " 'Course if you was to climb into that big Monarch, that red diesel job over there, if you was to climb in without my seeing you and I found you in the seat, I couldn't very well throw a man out in the middle of the desert, could I?"

They pulled out onto the road, the man at the wheel peering steadily ahead down the highway. "My name's Scotty Williams," he grunted. "What's yours?"

"Bob Longe."

"I knew you were from the East the moment I set eyes on ya back there."

"Yes, sir . . . I mean, Scotty. . . ." Somehow *Mister* didn't suit him. "Why, yes, Scotty. My home is about forty miles from New York."

"That's really something. Hiking across the U.S. with a set of golf clubs. Not many kids would have the nerve." Robin was silent. It hardly seemed necessary to explain the clubs were along because of a mistake. "Where you heading, Mac?"

"Oh, I dunno, exactly. California, I guess. I've always wanted to see California."

"Boy, you struck pay dirt! I'm headed straight for Oakland. You're sure lucky. Usually I have a helper along and we take turns sleeping in back there. But he's a wino. He's back in K.C."

"A wino? What's that?"

"Likes wine. Once in a while he mixes it with whiskey. Then . . . out! But I get double for the trip, so I don't mind."

"Oh, I see. You sleep in the truck?"

"No, right behind the seat here. The truck's full of frozen meat; it's refrigerated. I'd freeze if I slept in there. Just behind me there's a regular sleeping compartment like on a train. We highball right through, eight hours on, eight hours off. When one guy is driving, the other can stretch out and sleep."

"If he can," laughed Robin, as the truck swayed down the road.

"Oh, you get used to it."

The machine, a huge jointed monster with the driver's cab and engine in front and an enclosed trailer behind, roared along at an increasing speed and with increasing noise. Directly in front of Robin's seat was a metal plaque which read:

Western Freight Lines System
Warning
Insurance on this vehicle cannot be termed
in force when traveling at speeds in excess of
50 miles per hour

Involuntarily Robin leaned over and glanced at the speedometer. It was pointed at sixty-five and quivering upward, for the truck was gaining speed every second. Immediately he wished he hadn't, because the gesture seemed impolite, a kind of questioning of the driver's judgment.

The man at the wheel, however, took no notice of it. Then an insistent honking from behind penetrated the roar and rattle of the cab. It grew louder and louder, rose higher still, and finally a car drew up beside them, the horn going furiously.

Scotty leaned from the window toward the passing automobile. It was a lovely blue convertible driven by a young chap of about Robin's age. The top was down, and the driver signaled as he went past.

"Aw, go fry yer hat," said Scotty, while the other car moved ahead. It gained slowly, however, for the truck was thundering along at a fast pace.

"Those young punks," he went on, scorn in his tone. "Once they manage to promote a license for themselves, they know all there is to know about driving. They can tell folks who've been on the road thirty years how to drive." This was somewhat reminiscent of remarks Robin had heard his father make, so he kept silent.

Scotty drove on some miles before he spoke again. "We better stick to Number Six a while yet. Then pretty soon I want to take a rest. Number Six is murder over those passes right now; the road's all up. I'd rather go the long way, it's shorter in the end."

The highway curved and rose gradually. More mountains came into sight on both sides. The scenery was grander; every minute peaks appeared, some capped with snow. Robin was excited; these were the first really high mountains he had ever seen except for the Continental Divide.

Scotty, who traveled this route several times a month, pointed out the various summits to be seen from the passing truck. "That-there big baby, that's Gunnison Butte. The big boy ahead on the right, that's Gray Head. Nine thousand feet above sea level, that one is. Pretty soon we'll pass the roadside geyser; you should oughta see that. Then in a while we'll be on Soldier Summit, almost seven thousand. We hit a good spot, we'll stop for a little chow."

To think I could have missed all this, thought Robin, speechless. I almost quit the time I had to stay that night under the bridge and again this morning in the sun outside Denver. I'm plenty glad I stuck it. You have to stay with a thing of this kind. It sure isn't fun at times, he admitted to himself as he looked across the clear air toward the snow-capped peaks on the horizon, but it's sure worth it.

"You make this road a lot, don't you, Scotty?" he asked.

"Twice a month, son. Twice a month I'm between San Francisco and Omaha or Kansas City. We operate regular routes on a time schedule, just like any common carrier, just like the Santa Fe. We carry twenty tons of freight. . . ."

"Twenty tons! Why, that's . . . that's . . ."

"Forty thousand pounds, Mac," said the driver promptly, "that's right. Forty thousand back there right now. That baby behind has a fourteen hundred cubic-foot load; we can carry enough furniture for two large homes."

Robin was impressed. Now towns flashed past at

intervals, towns that were often only a filling station and a few wooden shacks, towns with names like Long Pine, Red Gulch, Powderhorn. The smaller the place, the more likely it was to be named a city. Carson City, Greenwood City, Canyon City were crossroads, with little more than a store that was also a post office. The rivers fascinated him. Bullfrog Creek, Minnie Maud Creek, Wild Horse Creek were only dry sandy beds now in the summer drought. But there were bigger streams: the Colorado, the Green, the Muddy. It was exciting to be crossing this wonderful country with a companion who knew the region and stories about the people and places they passed.

Shortly after six they stopped for food in a tiny place called Guide Rock. There actually were horses hitched outside the café between the parked cars. Inside, it was a smallish room filled with big men in wide-brimmed hats. Now I'm in the West; this is the real West, thought Robin. Scotty found a seat at one end of the long counter, and Robin edged onto an empty stool at the other end. The boss was making change for a man at his side, handing out four silver dollars. It was not the first time Robin had seen them, but never before had he seen four at one time.

He noticed a sign on the wall: *Franks, 25 cents.* Twenty-five cents for a frankfurter! It seemed a lot of money, especially when your cash was running low and you probably wouldn't be able to earn more until you hit a golf course on the Coast. One frank for twenty-five cents!

Timidly he remarked to the man who stood wiping the counter with one corner of his greasy apron, "That right there? Twenty-five cents for a frank?"

Before the counterman could answer, a big rancher on the next stool tapped his shoulder. "You from the East, ain't ya, bud?"

Robin nodded. He wished he hadn't started anything. He hated above all to feel conspicuous, and the entire counter was straining to get a look at him. He could see faces peering out all up and down the line. Before he could say anything he was smacked on the back. The blow stunned him; in fact, it nearly knocked him off the stool and into the astonished counterman.

"Son, you're in the West now! Sam, give this boy three franks and a coffee on me."

Bob chokingly thanked him and the man smiled. "Don't need no thanks, son. You're in the West now. We do that for strangers all the time." A chorus of approval greeted this remark, the men turned back to their meals, and Robin gradually recovered his composure.

Before long he and Scotty were back on the road again, traveling at a rapid speed. Robin once again glanced at the speedometer, which hovered around seventy.

This time Scotty noticed the glance. "Yeah . . . yeah, well, I always hold her down when I have passengers along. Once, when I was a lot younger, I wanted to see my girl in San Carlos and I went from Denver to San Francisco in twenty-three and a half hours. Twelve hundred and seventy miles—no stops, no meals, no sleep, nothing. That's moving, Mac, over these roads."

Robin had to agree. Some miles farther along Scotty slowed down. A few cars were parked beside the road ahead, and people were standing around. As they drew near, it became evident that there had been an accident, and one car could be seen badly smashed in front. A state trooper stood taking notes beside the car. Two people were stretched on the ground. Scotty came slowly to a stop, leaned from his cab, and shouted across the road, "Anyone killed?"

"No . . . no . . . just some folks badly shaken up."

"Oh," he said, looking at the unconscious figures stretched on the ground beside the highway. Then his interest immediately faded, he put the truck in gear, and they moved on again up the road.

Chapter 13

DAWN came slowly up behind them. Directly ahead the peaks were pink and glowing in the reflection of the rising sun. It was a magnificent sight, like nothing Robin had ever seen before. They thundered along, down toward a huge lake and into a town called Provo. On the outskirts Scotty drew up at one of his favorite restaurants for a big breakfast. Robin found he was hungry; also that the meal was expensive.

Once on the road again, Scotty explained that he knew how to avoid the traffic of Salt Lake City, and before many hours they were headed across the desert. The mountains were in the distance now; the road was the flattest and straightest Robin had ever seen.

Gradually, as the hours passed, the trucker became more talkative. "What school you go to, Mac? Going to Yale, hey? That's a fine place," he remarked, much to Robin's amazement. Then he started on golf. "What's your score, son?"

"Well . . . my best . . . I guess my usual round

is about 80 or 82. I did break 80 on our course at home. What do you shoot?"

"Me? Oh, let's see. When I was playing back there, when I was in tournaments, I was breaking 70."

"You mean you played in golf tournaments? You're a tournament player?"

Scotty lighted a cigarette deftly with one hand, holding about fifty thousand pounds of steel and cargo on the road with the other. He laughed at his passenger's surprised tone. "Why, sure. I played a little before I went in stir."

Robin gasped. What next? First you meet a truck driver who is a tournament golfer and breaks 70; then he turns out to have a criminal record. Jail did not mean quite the same thing to Robin that it had meant before he left home, but it was a shock to discover his kindly and agreeable companion had been in prison. He looked at him with a new curiosity.

"You mean to say . . . you mean you've really been in jail?" The words were out before he could stop himself.

Scotty took the question calmly. His tone was casual. "Oh, sure. I served a term awhile back. Guess I married too many women." He paused, then added, "At the same time."

"Oh. I see," said Robin, gasping again. He decided to change the subject. "But where d'you play tournament golf? In the East?"

"Back home in St. Paul. I was city champion and hit the Public Parks twice."

"The what?" Robin felt he knew golf. He read the sport pages; he had heard about the Open and the Amateur, the Masters and the Western, the Trans-Mississippi and the Tam O'Shanter. But this was a new one.

Scotty shot him a glance full of scorn. "Don't you know golf, Mac? That's the biggest tournament on earth; often has fifteen thousand entries. See now, a fella plays the public course in his home town; then the winners meet for the U.S. title."

"Oh, I didn't know." He was learning all the time, and apparently to learn about golf you had to cross the continent, reach Nevada, and fall in with a truck-driving golf star. The United States was a strange place. He understood why it had sometimes puzzled Hugh Gathwick. "How d'you make out, Scotty?"

"Not so bad. Semifinals twice, finals once," he replied mechanically. Robin realized he had been asked this question a hundred times, just as folks always asked him whether he was related to Bob Longe, the old Yale pole vaulter. "First crack I was in the semis. Then next time I was beaten in the finals in Chicago in thirty-seven holes by this guy Kennedy. Ever hear of him?"

Robin thought quickly. "Yes, of course. Buck

Kennedy. He did pretty well in the Amateur last year or was it two years ago, didn't he?"

"That's the one. Yep, he did all right for himself. Well, I lost to Bucky on the thirty-seventh at Edgemore. Missed a putt by a quarter inch. Next year I was conked by a plumber from Fort Worth, Texas. There was a guy from the West somewhere, a car dealer from Grand Rapids, and this plumber and me all in the semifinals that year at Knoxville. Fine bunch of guys. Well, that's America for you, Mac."

Robin was dazed. A public parks tournament with plumbers and truck drivers competing, with fifteen thousand entries, and he had never heard of it. Where have I been? he wondered. "What d'you say you shot?"

"In the finals that time? Oh, I forget now. That was a tough one to lose. I haven't played much lately. Golf's a game you must keep at all the time; you must practice and keep on practicing."

Then came another discovery. Robin expected Scotty to tell about his big matches in detail as they roared across the Great Salt Lake Desert. Not at all. The man at the wheel seemed to feel quite casual about the game of golf, and he soon began discussing road transport and the high taxes that trucking companies had to pay in every state they entered. Like most good golf players, he refused to talk much about himself or his game. The lesson was impressed on Robin, who recalled he had never heard his father

go into detail about his victories in the Intercollegiates or the Olympics, either.

It was late that night when finally they reached
the outskirts of Reno. Scotty parked the truck beside the road and prepared to lie down in the little
compartment behind the cab to rest awhile. Robin
was not sleepy, so he decided to visit the town and
meet his friend later at a gas station they agreed
upon. The truck driver stopped a pal, who oblig-
ingly deposited Robin two blocks from the center
of the town.

Robin walked over to the main street. Just to be
up and around at twelve-fifteen in the morning
seemed exciting. Although it was after midnight,
everything was open, stores were crowded, people
jammed the streets, and the night clubs with the glaring neon signs seemed full. He asked a question of
two boys standing on a street corner, got talking with
them, and discovered they were both juniors at the
University of Nevada. They were interested to meet
a hitchhiker from the East and gave him plenty of
information about the city.

A truck went past full of garbage cans that rattled
and clinked as it moved down the broad street.
"Those cans are full of silver dollars," remarked one
boy.

"Silver dollars?"

"Yes, they're taking them to the bank. Some banks
stay open all night to receive them. One reason the

night clubs use silver dollars is to prevent holdups. Fella couldn't move very fast with a hundred silver dollars on him."

After a while the three stopped in a drugstore for a drink, and Robin learned that gambling was legal in Nevada, that the night clubs were usually open until morning. The two boys offered him a bed in their fraternity house for the remainder of the night, and for just a moment he began to feel tired and considered their hospitality. However, this meant hitching another ride to the Coast, and as he was well fixed with Scotty he refused their offer with thanks.

Very well then, they insisted, if he was going straight on to San Francisco, he should at least see something of the town. They argued for five minutes as to which night club he ought to visit. Minors were not admitted, but some were stricter than others. At last they decided to try the Sans Souci.

The Sans Souci gave no trouble whatever. It was a huge place on the main street, packed with people even though it was almost one in the morning. Tables of all sorts were scattered about the big room, and hundreds of slot machines were lined against the wall, sounding off with riflelike blasts. The three boys circulated around the tables, and the two Nevada boys explained the various games to Robin. For a while he looked on at roulette, baccarat, and faro tables. After some time he wandered over to the slot machines. They fascinated him.

He had been standing there a few moments when he noticed a most attractive dark-eyed girl nearby. He thought she glanced at him and smiled slightly. He looked at her again and saw that indeed she was smiling. Being a stranger in Reno, however, he knew the smile could not be meant for him and he turned around. There was no one near.

He looked again quickly. Could she be smiling at him? Yes . . . she was. She smiled once more now and he liked it, although it made him feel queer for some reason.

Then she spoke. "Hello, stranger," she said, sauntering toward him.

He hoped fervently that his friends were not watching. Most certainly she was an attractive lady, though unlike Pamela and his partners at school dances. His roommate at Taft would have called her an interesting piece of furniture. She had an air about her that those girls lacked, an amusing smile, pretty dark eyes. Older than the girls he knew and somehow prettier, too. He tried to respond to her greeting. His throat was dry, and for a moment the words refused to come. For no reason at all he began to tremble. He couldn't understand why he should tremble so.

"Want to try your luck?" She nodded toward the machines.

Apparently she had not noticed his trembling, so he decided he was making an impression on the lady. He reflected a moment. His parents had forbidden him to drink but they had said nothing about gambling in a Reno night club. Besides, gambling was legal in Nevada. And was playing a slot machine gambling, anyhow? He became suddenly confused. But although he was not sure what he should do and although he was low on funds, he decided he could risk a quarter. Yes, he certainly might risk one quarter. After all, he would never be in Reno again. But just one quarter, not a cent more.

"O.K. Why not?" He smiled at her, feeling a good deal of a rake. She smiled back and moved considerably closer to him, much closer in fact. He rather enjoyed feeling her leaning against his shoulder.

Shoving in his quarter, he pulled the handle of the machine. Suddenly there was an amazing noise, a queer, clanking sound, one he had never heard before. Then out came rushing and clattering dozens of silver quarters that piled up in the tray below.

The girl jumped with excitement. "You hit the jack pot! You hit it the first time! Brother, are you lucky! I'll stay with you, big boy, you're sure lucky." She clapped her hands and danced with excited pleasure. She could not have been more pleased if the money had been her own.

Robin was quite as excited as she was, and with elation he scooped the pile of quarters from the tray in the machine. They filled both trouser pockets and overflowed into the pockets of his jacket till it sagged down on both sides.

She took his arm and, pressing closer, steered him toward another machine farther down the line. This, he observed immediately, was a fifty-cent machine.

"Here, try this one," she said.

He hesitated. "No, once is enough," he said firmly. "Besides, I'm hitching west. I need that dough."

She turned, her mouth open, and dropped his arm. For a moment she stared at him, amazement on her face. Then, to his surprise, she came closer and patted him tenderly on the cheek. "Oh . . . you're cute. You're really sweet. You make me think of my son. He's a freshman at Southern Cal."

Chapter 14

AS they pulled out of Reno shortly before dawn, Scotty revealed the passion of his life—diesels. While the truck followed the twisting uphill road, he explained this was a new job, hardly two months old, and with enthusiasm in his voice he went on to explain the principle upon which the engine worked.

"Now a diesel . . . you take a diesel built by G.M., boy, you got something. Y'see, in a diesel engine the air and fuel are self-ignited through the heat of compression. The air does as much work as the fuel. So what? You use less fuel. It's more efficient and less expensive than an ordinary gas engine."

Robin was not mechanical; to him, Butch had seemed a wizard who did things with engines that were miraculous. Moreover, he had been up two nights in a row, so it was difficult to stay awake. Scotty's words came to him through a haze of fatigue.

"Just an internal combustion engine . . . see now, the generated heat ignites the fuel . . ."

Despite every effort, Robin's head nodded. He fell back exhausted, and finally Scotty let him alone.

Suddenly the hydraulic brakes gripped, snorted, shook the cab, and brought Robin sharply to life again. They were in a thick pine forest now, descending a curve to a small ravine. Beyond, the highway wound sharply uphill as far as he could see.

"Smells to me sorta like a fire."

"A fire!" Robin was only half awake. "A fire? I don't get it."

"Yeah." The trucker sniffed. "Now you do."

Robin pulled himself together but smelled nothing. On they went, up, up around a curve. Then the pungent odor assailed him. "Oh, yes, sure. Now I smell it. I sure do."

"Forest fire somewhere up ahead, that's for certain. I often smell 'em coming through these forests but never as close as this. We're headed into it, too." As if to confirm his remark, a bus, honking wildly, roared past them. Inside were several dozen grimy-looking citizens, a few of whom waved at Scotty as they shot past.

"Yes, sir, I was right, Mac. They're bringing up the fire crews."

Robin sat up. This was a new and interesting turn of events. "Tell me, Scotty, what about these fire crews? Where do they come from?"

"Oh, from all over. Those in that bus were mostly hobos, Reno pickups. The real smoke-eaters, the pros, come from the California side."

"Are we pretty near the line now?"

"Yes, not too far. Just a few miles beyond here. We'll rise two-three thousand feet now in an hour or more."

Indeed it was slow, upgrade work. Cars kept shooting past them, all giving evidence of the seriousness of the fire and the preparations that were being made. Trucks went by carrying fire equipment: tools, axes, rakes, saws. Occasionally they saw private automobiles full of ranchers who were evidently volunteers. Once a large kitchen on wheels rumbled past, smoke issuing from its stovepipe. This was followed by a truck stacked with provisions: boxes of food, bags of oranges, sacks of potatoes, piled-up K-rations.

Robin became more and more interested. He hoped they wouldn't miss it, that it would not be over by the time they reached it. But the smoky sky evidenced a widespread fire. "Think we'll get a look at it from the highway, Scotty?"

Scotty lit a cigarette with one hand, swinging his vast machine round a curve with the other. "How can we miss? That smoke up there . . . get it? You can see it plainly now. That's on the Donner."

"The Donner? What's that?"

The driver shot him a scornful look. "I keep forgetting you're from the East, Mac," he snorted. "You never did hear of the Donner Pass, I s'pose? Well, it's the main road between Reno and Sacramento over the mountains, and at one point it's up above seven thousand feet. Years ago there was a big party of pioneers got snowed in there one winter and froze to death. Why, just awhile back a crack Union Pacific train got stuck there, couldn't go forward nor back. Three days, it was, three days it took the rescue parties to get the passengers out."

Robin became sober. This was rugged country. He began to appreciate their height by the fact that even in the cozy cab of the truck he was chilly. He dug round in back, found his suitcase, and pulled on his sweater.

"Yes, sir, that's a real big one up ahead," said Scotty.

A siren sounded and a state road-patrol car, loaded down with troopers in uniform, tore past, zoomed dangerously around a curve ahead, and disappeared.

The siren shrieked on in the distance. "Them guys sure in a hurry. Things must be getting worse, wherever it is," remarked Scotty. They kept moving higher, occasionally dipping down into smoke-filled pockets, where small fires burned on both sides of the road and blackened trees showed where the blaze had been stopped.

Then they rounded a long, wide turn to find a line of cars and trucks reaching ahead as far as they could see. A man in khaki uniform with a green pine-tree badge on the pocket of his jacket came toward them holding up one hand. "State of emergency!" he shouted. "All men report at once. State of emergency! Get out there, you two truckers. We need you up ahead on the Pass."

Robin was amazed at the speed with which Scotty reacted. He reached back and found a small canteen that he slung over his shoulder. Then he opened a door into the rear compartment, disclosing a rumpled bed with some clothes tossed on it.

"Take off your sweater," he ordered. "Put on these coveralls of Joe's." He yanked them out and tossed them to Robin. They were greasy, dirty, caked with grime.

Robin was repelled. "I guess I'll be all right. I don't think . . ."

"Put 'em on. Do what I tell ya. Leave that sweater here."

"But, Scotty, I'm cold."

"Ya won't be long, fella. Put on those high boots of his. You'll kill yourself in those shoes out in the forest."

Robin obeyed, though it seemed foolish. He removed his sweater, climbed into the greasy coveralls, laced the boots, and climbed down from the truck. Scotty locked both sides carefully and went round to the back to be sure that was locked also.

Meanwhile, the man in khaki uniform was arguing with a young fellow in a Lincoln convertible that had pulled up behind them. "Look, Mister, I'm not *asking* you, I'm *telling* you. We need every bit of help we can get. This thing is dangerous. You're wanted up there on the Pass. Get out!"

"Listen!" said the driver of the Lincoln. "My father is the president of the First National Bank of Sacramento. I've got to get through to Sacramento tonight. Sorry, but I can't stop, fire or no fire."

"Mister, I wouldn't care if your father was President, period. I'm the chief supervisor of the Forest Service in this district, and I'm empowered by law to make arrests. This is an emergency and every able-bodied man helps. Do you help or do I turn you over to the state cops?"

Grumbling, the young man got out of his Lincoln, and the Forest Service man moved along to the next car. His voice was hoarse and tired. "State of emergency! State of emergency! All men report at once. That means you three guys in that Oldsmobile with the Kansas license!"

Golly, thought Robin, I'd have missed this if I'd quit back there in Denver. I might never have had a chance to fight a forest fire, a real Western forest fire. Won't this be something to write to Mother about!

There was not much time to think. They were all piled into a passing truck which was already full, and were jounced, bounced, and rocked up past the long line of cars for several miles. By the chill in the air Robin realized they must be reaching the top of the pass, although the smoke was so thick little could be seen. As they went past the cars, he noticed that only women were standing in the road beside them.

"All out! Snap into it, you guys!"

Robin jumped out and followed Scotty with excitement. Sleepiness vanished, fatigue was no longer in him; he was keen, alive, awake. This was surely something—fighting a forest fire on the Donner Pass. Am I lucky, he thought!

Tools were handed to each man—axes, grub hoes, rakes, saws. They seemed out of place in the hands of the well-dressed young fellow from the Lincoln and a few of the others.

A man in the uniform of the Forest Service addressed the group. "Men, this fellow here, Jake Dawson, is the fire boss. You're all under him. He's an old ranger, he's an experienced fire fighter. Been through all this a thousand times, haven't you, Jake? Do exactly what he says and don't worry. He knows the forests. Now get moving. Get us some action out there."

They stepped out in single file through the woods along a narrow trail. It was a queer crew: tourists in summer sports clothes, Mexicans, truck drivers both black and white, hobos who hadn't shaved in weeks, young chaps in flannels and white shirts, older men who looked like the salesmen who had so often given Robin lifts between Rochester and Reno. They moved on, some puffing and grunting already. Beside a clearing in the woods, figures rolled up in blankets were sleeping soundly. Robin realized that the fire must have been under way for some days.

On, on, up, up, until finally they stepped out into the clear on a rocky ledge. There they stopped. Across a canyon was the fire—a horrible, menacing thing, creeping steadily toward them, swallowing everything in its path: trees, bushes, undergrowth. It could be seen leaping from treetop to treetop in the wind. High pines roared up toward the sky.

Say, this is no picnic, Robin thought. This is serious.

Scotty stood beside him. "Must have been going for days. It's a crown fire now. That takes the tops of the highest trees, jumps from one to another . . . like that . . . there . . . see over there!" While they watched, the tallest pines across the ravine became flaming towers, their smoke reaching into the sky.

A voice rasped at them. "All right, you guys. You're not here to watch. You'll see plenty before long. Here's where the line starts, so get busy."

The men began to hack away, clearing the underbrush, scraping off the small stuff, cutting away the lower branches, chopping down trees, laying bare the ground for a space eight feet wide, to hold back the oncoming conflagration. Robin was working with a tool that was a combination hoe on one side and a sort of hooked rake on the other.

"Fire lines like these is no good in this wind,"

growled someone near him. "A crown fire can jump an eight-foot line like you jump that little brook down there."

They could feel the warm air from the flames as they worked, and Robin realized that the fire was getting closer, because the heat was increasing. Minutes passed, an hour, another hour, and still they hacked, chopped, raked, and sawed to make that fire line along the hilltop.

Robin was amazed to discover that some of the worst-looking bums with beards four days old could handle an ax and a saw better than he could. They were at it as hard as ever when his back had begun to ache and his arms felt like lead. Sweat poured out all over him. Now he understood why Scotty had forced him to leave his sweater in the truck. The dry wind parched his lips. He kept licking them, but still they were dry and brittle.

Thick black smoke whirled and eddied through the air; charred bits of wood sailed high and then, carried by the wind across the canyon, dropped at their feet. The burning embers started blazes which had to be snuffed out with the backs of shovels immediately. You worked to hold one fire, and while your back was turned another burst out behind you. Here and there a man tumbled to the ground. One or two sat propped against trees, entirely spent. Among them was the son of the Sacramento bank president, grimy, panting, utterly exhausted.

Another hour, and the fire was sweeping down the ravine and eating its way up their side of the hill. Now the red glare dazzled Robin's eyes and he could feel the terrific heat on his face. Scotty extended the canteen. Robin found himself grabbing it eagerly, drinking the clear water, trying to wash the smoke from his mouth and throat.

A gang of loggers passed, every one too spent for words. Slowly, steadily, the fire came up toward the crest, reaching around the sides, licking little tongues here and there out behind them. Men looked anxiously toward the fire boss, wondering whether he was taking chances, waiting eagerly for the word to jump and run.

The excitement, the fun, the thrill of it had gone. Now it was grim, hard work. And this line they were trying to hold was only one tiny segment of the vast fire that must cover hundreds of acres. Great trees across the ravine still blazed like huge torches, sending sparks in every direction. Sudden, ominous blasts of heat assailed them. The actual fire was dangerously close now.

Robin glanced at his watch. It was early afternoon. Scotty's eyes were bloodshot, his face was black with soot, one sleeve of his gray shirt was ripped away, his hat had vanished. Robin ran the back of his hand across his own face. It was black with soot also.

"Everyone out! Everybody out!" shouted the boss. He stood counting carefully as the men filed past:

"Twenty-one, twenty-two, twenty-three . . ." The banker's son stumbled. His shoes were split open, his clothing torn to tatters. "Twenty-four . . . twenty-five. Get back quick, down the trail. This fire line isn't going to hold. Everyone's checked. Let's go!"

The banker's son was falling back. Scotty stopped, put his arm under his shoulders, and helped him stumble over the rocks and charred earth.

Well, their work had been useless. The fire had licked them. Robin hated to quit, hated to leave the flames in possession of the hilltop. Yet there was nothing else to be done. Now they would have to fall back and make another, perhaps a wider fire line farther along.

The banker's son was heavy. He was soft and flabby, and in his state of collapse he leaned on Scotty more and more. A few others stumbled and fell and had to be helped down the trail. Sparks and cinders showered down on them. Now and then a burning pine cone, carried by heavy gusts of wind, started a fire in the underbrush near them.

Then it came. It came without any warning whatever. All day the smoke and the thick haze had obscured the sky, so they had seen nothing of the heavens. Suddenly rain fell, a trickle at first, a few drops, then more, faster, heavier. It was a joyful and complete surprise, a sail appearing to shipwrecked men alone on the ocean, water in the desert. It was relief, succor, rescue, the only thing that could possibly stop that encroaching wall of flame roaring across the mountains in the wind.

In hoarse tones they laughed, yelled, cheered, shouted. By the time they had finally stumbled down to the highway, the rain was a torrent against which no fire on earth could compete. Faces relaxed. The Forest Service men smiled at last. Folks crept gleefully back into their cars for shelter, repairing damage to body and clothes as best they could.

Scotty turned the banker's son over to a first-aid outfit, and he and Robin walked slowly down toward their truck in the downpour. They were far too beaten to walk fast, even in the stinging rain. Just above the truck they passed a kitchen and an emergency chow line. It was five o'clock and they stopped, for Scotty said it might be hours before traffic would move again. Robin stood between two seedy-looking characters. Just below were a couple of Mexican laborers jabbering away in Spanish. Ahead of them three Negro truckers, their uniforms in shreds, stood laughing in the rain. They had all been out on the fire lines. They seemed like brothers to Robin now.

The hot stew, a dish he detested at home, seemed the most perfect meal he had ever tasted. The bitter coffee brought solace to his parched throat. They finished slowly, standing together in the downpour, feeling the water on their bare heads, rejoicing in the spatter of rain on the concrete.

"Gee, Mac, are you a sight!" remarked Scotty, as they neared the truck.

He unlocked the doors and Robin swung up into the cab. It was like coming home after a long journey. He felt years older than when he had stepped down to the pavement into a great adventure. His face was burned by sparks, his hands were scratched and bloody, there was a cut on one arm where a tree branch had torn the coveralls and penetrated the skin. He was dirty, exhausted, beaten, bushed. Yet somehow, as he sank onto the seat, he felt exultant. He had been living during those past hours.

Chapter 15

WHEN Scotty finally dropped him that foggy morning in Oakland, Robin had less than eight dollars in his pocket. Cross-country travel, he had discovered, is expensive even when the transportation is free. Obviously it was necessary to build up his bank roll at once. The first thing he looked for was a telephone.

Eight dollars! That's cutting things close, he thought, as he searched the telephone book. If this turned out to be Denver all over again, if the Blakes were away too, he saw nothing for it but another siege of dish washing. Unless he was lucky enough to hook on at some golf club.

Fortunately there was only one Bruce G. Blake in the San Francisco telephone book. Robin had asked for no names or addresses before leaving, and his father had offered none. This name, however, was fixed in his memory. Ever since he could remember he had heard of Bruce Blake, captain of the football team and Dad's roommate at New Haven.

He tried hard to stress his whole name when the girl answered the ring. "Bob Longe, Third," he said, as plainly as he could. However, the masculine voice that immediately came on the phone was excited. "Bob, old boy, it isn't really you! What on earth are you doing out here, old-timer?"

"No, sir, it's not my father. It's me, Bob."

"Oh, I see . . . I see. Well, mighty happy to hear from you, son. Where are you?"

"I'm at Oakland, at the ferry terminal."

"Good. That's just fine. Now I tell you what to do. Take the ferry, walk up Market Street, and come to my office—five hundred and fifty. Got it? We'll go have some lunch as soon as you get here."

Well, thought Robin as he rang off, there's a free meal anyway, and right at this point that's important. Actually, it was a lot more than a free meal. It was the Haskells and Evanston and Skokie all over again. Mr. Blake insisted on his staying at their home near Burlingame, where he introduced Bob to his two boys, Tim and Andy. Andy was a sophomore at New Haven; Tim was a senior in high school. He was caddying for the summer at the country club, and it was easy for him to introduce Bob to the pro and put him to work.

The first thing Tim did was to lend him a sweater and some warm clothes. To Bob's amazement, mornings in August were not warm in California. For a solid week he spent every day, all day, on the golf course. When he was not caddying, he was out on the practice field. It was good to return to golf, to get the feel of his clubs once more. He even enjoyed listening to the other caddies talk about California and her chances in the Pacific Conference that fall and discuss colleges like Fresno State, Pomona, and Occidental, whose names he had never heard before.

During his off moments Bob put in some concentrated practice and soon found his touch returning. He started to hit balls that brought an astonished whistle from Tim Blake. It was easy for him, he liked the game; it seemed to present none of the toil and effort and concentration that pole vaulting did. With no great show of strength, he could smack drives that fairly whistled down the fairways.

Once he heard the pro, standing behind him near the caddie house, remark to his assistant, "Say! Looka that new kid, that boy with the Blakes. He's a loosy-goosy up there."

"He sure is. I watched him yesterday. Why, he's so loose he can tie a knot in himself. Never saw anything like it."

A few hours later the pro accosted him. "Son, where d'you play at home?"

"Me? Why, I play Sweet Briar, in Connecticut."

"You could be a golfer with some work and practice," the pro said matter-of-factly.

His heart jumped. "Gee! You really mean it?

That's great; I love golf. I'd rather play golf than anything."

"Well, stay with it. Let me see, you're with the Blakes, aren't you? Stick around the next six weeks or so and I'll help you. I'll make a player out of you."

"I sure wish I could, but I have to think of getting home again soon."

"You're due back East, are you? Then why don't you play the Junior Championships at Detroit on your way? That's just a suggestion."

"The Junior Championships? I never thought about it. I'd sure like to try. When is it?"

"Well, it's the twenty-eighth of this month at Oakland Hills. How old are you? Sixteen? Tell you what, son, let me have a couple of dollars for your entry fee, and I'll fill out the blank and certify to your age and send it along. Then if you *should* want to stop off and play on your way home, you can. What you got to lose?"

It sounded sensible, so he gave the money to the pro, the exact facts about his age and so on, and then forgot it. The following Monday was caddies' day at the club. There was a small tournament each week for the boys, as there had been at Skokie, with a box of balls as first prize.

The pro came up just before Bob drove off. "I'm anxious to see what you do today. Y'know, this is really a tough course. They played the Open here four years ago and the fellows all agreed it was one of the hardest they'd ever tackled."

Actually, Bob's score was high; the course really was hard. But this was all fun for him. He could haul off and smack the ball two hundred and fifty yards into the distance with ease, or lay his seven iron a few inches from the flag. Anyone can play this game, he thought.

The pro urged him to stay on, but Bob knew he should be moving. Hitchhiking across a continent takes time, and there were three thousand miles to be covered before he could see Five Mile River again. His mother's letters were full of inquiries as to when he could be expected, and suggestions about sending him money to return by air.

He found the Blakes hard to leave, but he wanted to ride down the coast and look at Los Angeles. So, with sixty-two dollars in his pocket, he started the long trek homeward one morning. Regretfully the Blakes took him to Route Number One, the main coastal highway, and said good-by.

It seemed familiar to be standing at the side of the road while the Plymouths and Pontiacs, the Fords and Chevvies went past in that dizzy procession. Whoosh . . . whoosh . . . whoosh! He had hardly been there five minutes, arm extended and a smile on his face, when a car screeched to a stop ahead and backed toward him. The door opened and out stepped an elegant state trooper, hat over his eyes, gun on his hip. The smile quickly left Bob's face.

"Where d'you think you're going, young fella?"

"Home," replied Bob truthfully.

"Yeah? Where's that?"

"Five Mile River, Connecticut."

"You sure got some ways to go. What's your name?"

"Robert B. Longe."

The trooper looked him over. "I kinda figured you was from the East. Don't you know there's a law against hitchhiking in this state?"

"No, sir, I really didn't."

"Well, you sure do now. Let's see your papers." He held out his hand impatiently while with clumsy fingers Bob searched for his driver's license and his school cards. At last he dug them out and handed them over. Half a dozen cards fell to the ground and blew around. Furious with himself, with the trooper, with California law, he scurried after them.

The cop glanced at his license, turned the cards over, handed them back. "You been in the army?"

In Iowa, Colorado, California, the cops all seemed to ask the same questions. "No, not yet. I'm sixteen. You can see there. It's printed on the license here . . . see?"

The trooper glanced at it again. "Oh. We get a

lot of deserters out here. Not running away from home, are you?"

"I'm running toward home. I'm on my way home this minute. I have to be back in a couple of weeks."

"O.K. Got any money on you?"

Bob produced his purse and showed the sixty-two dollars. The cop looked at the money carefully and nodded. He turned, pulled a pad from his pocket, and walked toward his car. There, leaning on the front mudguard, he began to fill out some sort of a form. Presently he finished, closed the pad with a snap, replaced it in his hip pocket, and walked back, something green in his hand.

"This-here is merely a warning card, young fella. Three of 'em and we pick you up. If you didn't have cash with you, I could take you in as a vagrant right now. I advise you to stay off the roads in this state. Understand?"

Bob nodded and took the green card the trooper handed him. Then the man went back to his car, got in, made some more notes and finally, seeing a break in the long line of oncoming traffic, slipped out onto the highway.

Bob stood fingering the green card. Without a glance, he shoved it into his hip pocket. No hitch-hiking in California! Why hadn't the Blake boys told him? Why hadn't the kids around the caddie house at the country club mentioned it? Now what?

He stood concentrating, trying to figure his next move, wondering what he should do, flushed, angry, unhappy over the bad luck that had sent a state trooper along at that exact moment that morning. It was hard to know which way to turn. He hated to quit when he had gone so far through so many difficulties. But how could he go on?

Suddenly his golf bag toppled to the ground, and out slid his precious number four wood, a beautiful lithe club Dad had given him. On leaving home there had been a cover for this club, but somehow, somewhere along the way, the cover had been lost. It was his favorite club; he treasured it. Also he knew how to use it.

Hastily he reached down and picked up the club. Then, leaning his bag against the suitcase, he inspected the club head for scratches, wiped the dirt from it with the sleeve of his coat, and waved it casually through the air with one hand. Instantly, as if by magic, a car stopped just ahead. For a moment he thought it was another cop.

The car slid back and the man at the wheel opened the door. "Hurry up, son, hop in. Snap into it. I got to make Santa Barbara early this afternoon."

Bob piled in, smiling to himself, praying the cop was not coming back down the highway to see what was happening. Once again the day was sunny, the world was good, fortune favored him. Slamming the door, he stammered thanks.

"Glad to have you along, son. Fact is, I seldom pick up hitchhikers, especially here on Number One. But when I saw you swinging a club there, I just couldn't help myself. I have a boy about your age who plays, too. What's your score, son?"

Chapter 16

LOS ANGELES he found disappointing. After the deep beauty of San Francisco and the bay region, he felt it to be just another big American city, covered at times with an overhanging haze everybody called smog. The distances were too great for him to see much, the cost of living high.

There were no caddie jobs, and he felt he ought to get started homeward.

Yet he did not look forward to starting the long grind back to the East, especially in a state where there was a law against hitchhiking. However, he had to face it. On his last night he felt he ought to go out and really do the town. But he knew nobody in the vast metropolis and had no spare cash, so he settled for a cheap dinner and a movie. As he handed in his key at the desk of the Downtown Y., where he had a tiny cubbyhole for a room, the man behind the counter stared at him a moment and said, "Let's see, you're from Connecticut, aren't you?"

"Sure am. Why?"

"Got anything special on tonight?"

"Why, no, not exactly."

"Here's a ticket for the Tommy Dunn show, *Boom or Bust*. Biggest thing on the air out here. They send us a couple of tickets every week. They wanted a good-looking young chap from the East, and I guess you fill the bill."

It seemed to Robin as good a way as any other to spend the evening, and certainly an inexpensive way. Besides, he had always wanted to see a coast-to-coast broadcast. Urged by the man at the desk to arrive early, he settled for a hasty meal at a drugstore, hopped a bus, and reached the theater in Hollywood in plenty of time. When the doors were opened an hour later, a mob stampeded the place. Bringing up the rear, he was fortunate to get one of the few remaining seats, a place on the aisle in the next to the last row.

There was an enormous sign on the back curtain on the stage: *Tommy Dunn*. Underneath were the words *Boom or Bust*. Meanwhile, five or six elegantly dressed gentlemen with notebooks and pencils in their hands wandered up and down the aisle, looking the audience over carefully and with knowing gazes. Suddenly one leaned over and tapped his shoulder. "Where you from, Bud?"

"Five Mile River, Connecticut."

"Connecticut? Did you say Connecticut?"

"Yes, sir, that's right."

"You work in L.A.?"

"No, sir. I'm just here for a few days."

The man seized his shoulder and pulled. "Come with me." He led the way back and around the side, where a long curtain concealed a door in the wall. He opened it and they went up a flight of steps and were backstage.

Here everything was noise, dust, confusion, and excitement. People were rushing around aimlessly, shouting at each other. A glassed-in control room was at one end; men inside it were making strange signs to those outside. Robin noticed a shortish man with a large mustache and horn-rimmed glasses who was directing things, giving orders in nasal tones which everyone quickly obeyed. The young man yanked Robin by the arm and led him across the stage toward a girl in a light tan dress. She had red-dish hair, a good many freckles, was tall and well built.

The man introduced them hurriedly and left. The redhead smiled and said nothing. Robin felt dazed, hardly knowing what came next. One minute he had been quietly sitting as a member of the audience; now he was in the hubbub and uproar that precedes a coast-to-coast program. He was one of the participants. It gave him a slightly uneasy feeling.

The young man appeared, clutching a wad of notes and papers in his hand. "H'm, let's see. You're Miss . . . Miss Hayes . . . that's right." He checked her name on a pad. "You, young fella . . . you're

Mr. Longe. Good! You're the second couple. You start with twenty-five dollars, remember. You can put it all or any part of it you wish on each question. If you win on the first four questions, you're entitled to try for the Stickler. But only if you win all of the first four. Is that plain? D'you understand?"

Bob really did not understand, but apparently the girl did. She nodded serenely and smiled. Bob noticed her smile, a smile that lit up her face, and he decided she was by no means as homely as he had first imagined. She seemed to know what it was all about. Been through it before, he guessed.

Then sudden shouts, half subdued, came toward them. "On the air . . . on the air . . . we're on the air now." There was an immediate hush all around, and he heard a burst of applause from the other side of the curtain.

Right there he began to realize what he was up against. He turned to the girl. "Say . . . have we . . . do we have to go out there . . . before all those people?" He knew the answer perfectly well, but the idea frightened him.

The girl smiled reassuringly and laid her hand on his arm. "You won't mind, once you get out there. I'll help you. Besides, Tommy is lots of fun, really."

Again a burst of applause came from the other side of the curtain. It was followed by laughter that had a note of derision in it. It made him uncomfortable. He was sure he was not going to enjoy himself. These people in the audience were jeering at somebody, and he felt certain it was not Tommy Dunn.

Then the elegant young man, perspiring now and somewhat breathless, hurried toward them. "You're next, you're next," he whispered, taking the girl by the arm and leading them across to one side of the stage, where they stood behind a door in the wings. Bob's knees felt weak. He discovered he was leaning on a post for support. It annoyed him.

The man yanked his arm, opened the door, and pushed him onto the stage. The lights in front were so strong he could not see the people in the audience. However, he could hear them distinctly. A sort of murmur, a kind of titter rose as he groped across the endless stage and finally reached one of the two microphones placed for them, grabbing it for support. At an opposite microphone was the man with the whiskers, rubbing his hands at the sight of two new victims. He greeted them, while assistants leaned over and adjusted the microphones.

"Welcome, folks, welcome to *Boom or Bust*. Happy to have you here with us tonight. What's your name, young man?"

The question took Bob by surprise. The fact was that any question would have taken him by surprise. His mouth was completely dry, his throat parched, and he felt far worse than he had ever felt before the biggest track meet.

"Robert B. Longe, Third," he said, his voice cracking badly as he answered.

The titter was audible. He mopped his dripping forehead with a handkerchief that had been in his suit pocket ever since leaving home.

"Robert B. Longe, *Third*," said Whiskers, nodding eagerly. "I see. You play third base. What team, the Yanks?"

The whole theater rocked and roared with delight. It was not a very good jest but they loved it. Even the redhead smiled, which made things worse.

Bob flushed violently. He could have killed that grinning ape. After all, there were plenty of fellows at school with *Third* after their name, and even one or two with *Fourth*. His knees were trembling as they had at the night club in Reno, as they had that night under the bridge, and he was sure the audience must notice his fright. Yet when silence came, he replied quite calmly, although his voice was still high-pitched. "No, sir, if I was playing third base on the Yanks, I wouldn't likely be wasting my time on this program."

Laughter erupted again, not as loud or as lasting. This time, however, the laughter had no sting.

"Ouch!" said Whiskers. "Ouch! Wait a minute till I get this stiletto out of my chest. You're sharp, young fella. Where you from?"

"Five Mile River, Connecticut."

"Oh, I see. Here in God's country we'd call it Five

Thousand Mile River." This mild jest brought more laughter. "What-all brings you so far from home? Working on the Coast? Or d'you just like our western smog?"

Bob was forced to wait for another outburst of laughter to subside. These people, he decided, would laugh at almost anything. "No, sir, I'm just going through. I'm going to Yale . . ."

"Yale?" interrupted Whiskers, peering innocently through his spectacles. "Where's that?"

Again there was laughter. "In God's country," replied Bob. His knees were shaking somewhat less violently, although he still hated the whole thing. But as he talked, his normal voice came back. "In New Haven. That's a suburb of New York."

Once again the laughter exploded. Now the crowd was enjoying the duel between the older man and the youngster, and slowly Robin began to enjoy it too. Gradually he began to get control of himself. Maybe this was not so bad after all.

"Yale, hey?" Whiskers paused. "Yale. That's a rich man's school."

Robin turned quickly. "It is *not*," he protested with annoyance. By this time he was tired of this remark, which he had heard in various forms clean across the country. "Half the men are there on scholarships. What's more, it has a wider distribution of students geographically than California or Stanford or any other college in the United States.

Why, fellows come to New Haven from every single state in the Union."

Strange to stand there defending Yale, but he was not going to hear Dad's university run down on a radio program.

"Hey! I better watch my step," remarked Whiskers lamely, peering over his glasses again. "I suppose you're a football player?"

"No, sir, I pole-vault."

"I see. You jump through the air with the greatest of ease . . ."

"Well, not exactly, not with the greatest of ease," he interrupted, thinking of that shock when your pole hits the box and you start to rise, to twist, and turn up toward the bar.

"We have some mighty good pole vaulters and runners out here." Bob had noticed that these people were not exactly reluctant to talk about their teams and their champions. He had to admit they had plenty to discuss, too. "Out here, you know, if a two-day-old baby can't run the hundred in ten flat, we just chuck him back into the Pacific Ocean."

This was greeted with laughter and applause. Whiskers continued. "You drive out here from that New York suburb?"

"No, sir, I hitchhiked."

"You did, did you? That's strictly against the law in this state. I've a mind to hand you over to the police. Don't try any of that stuff on us, young fella."

Bob smiled. He wanted to hold up the green warning card but decided not to.

"Well, son, I imagine hitchhiking is a cheap way of seeing the U.S.A., isn't it?"

"Yes, sir. I have more money now than when I started." To his amazement, the entire audience applauded: At home nobody would have applauded. Nor would these people, perhaps, if they had known he had only about twenty dollars when he left home.

"You have, have you? Good for you. Mind my asking how much this trip has cost you since you left Connecticut?"

"Forty-two dollars and sixty-two cents," he answered promptly.

Again the audience applauded, and the girl beside him beamed. Bob felt warm and comfortable all over. Even his legs had stopped wobbling, so he spread them apart and casually put his hands behind his back.

"Wow!" said Whiskers, admiration in his tone. "That wouldn't take me to Santa Monica. What an operator! I'd like to ask one more question. What d'you eat on the road—birdseed?"

Once again the violent burst of applause. Reluctantly Robin had to admit the guy was good. He could make the sorriest jest sound amusing.

Then, with no warning, Whiskers turned on the girl. "Well, sister, what's your name?"

"Maryjanehayes." She said it so fast it all sounded like one word.

"Maryjanehayes." He imitated her so perfectly that the crowd roared with delight. "What d'you do, Maryjanehayes?"

She flushed ever so slightly at the noise but was sure of herself even in that laughter. "I'm a teacher at Long Beach," she said quietly.

"Ha, a teacher at Long Beach. I thought maybe you went to Harvard."

Applause and laughter rang out in the theater. She raised her eyebrows slightly but stood poised and steady, apparently not at all bothered by the audience or the japes. Bob glanced at her with interest. A teacher! In his experience, teachers seldom came equipped with the modern improvements possessed by this young lady.

"Well . . . well," resumed Whiskers, "enough of this. Let's get down to business. How much will you two bet on your first question? You started with twenty-five dollars, remember? How much will you bet?"

They turned and looked at each other. She had nice, friendly blue eyes. They twinkled a little. "Twenty-five," she whispered.

"Twenty-five," he said loudly. The audience immediately applauded.

"Good. You'll shoot the works. You'll go for the whole thing. This question ought to be easy for a Yale man. It's about colleges. Ready? Who are the Panthers?"

"Pittsburgh," said Bob.

"Arizona State," said the girl at the same moment.

"You're both correct," ejaculated Whiskers. "Actually, we should pay you double on that question. Now you have fifty dollars. How much will you bet on the second question?"

Yes, she certainly had nice eyes and long eyelashes, too. Bob looked at her searchingly. She nodded. Instantly he realized what she was saying.

"Fifty dollars."

"Good for you. Fifty dollars. Here's the question. Which is the Sunflower State?"

The Sunflower State? Sunflower State? Surely he had passed through it! He remembered . . . what states had he been through . . . Ohio . . . Illinois . . . Iowa . . . Kansas . . .

"Kansas!" he shouted.

"Right, Kansas." There was a burst of applause from the crowd and loud music from the orchestra. Whiskers needled him. "Any law against hitchhiking there, Mr. Yale?"

Bob flushed. "I really wouldn't remember."

"I wouldn't remember either if I were you," remarked Whiskers. "Now for the third question.

How much do you want to lay out this time? You have one hundred dollars now."

They looked at each other, their understanding perfect.

"One hundred," said Bob.

"Wonderful, wonderful! You'll risk the entire hundred. Very good, here is the third question. It's a history question. Ought to be easy for a student and a teacher. Who was the second president of the United States?"

"John Adams," they both said with delight, in unison.

"Two hundred. All right. Now here's the fourth question. How much will you put up?"

Plainly the questions were getting harder, yet the girl's look was steady and Bob hated to seem a piker, so he said, "Two hundred."

"You're sports. The whole two hundred. Ready for the question? How many sets of teeth has a horse?"

Silence. A long horrible silence followed. No quick and easy answer was coming from either of them. He glanced at the girl and saw from the dismay on her face that she was city-bred like himself and knew nothing about horses.

Sets of teeth . . . a horse . . . how many . . . I have two . . . a horse must have . . . take a chance . . . "Two," he said in desperation.

The music burst forth, the applause was sudden and loud, the crowd roared with delight. Now they were four hundred dollars ahead. Bob wiped his forehead with his handkerchief and turned toward the girl. She beamed at him.

"Fine work, fine work, splendid," said Whiskers. "Say, these Yale boys are really on the ball, aren't they? Now for the Stickler. This is the test question, the Stickler, and remember, folks, you do *not* have to answer it. You can quit now with your four hundred dollars or take a chance on the Stickler, just as you like. If you answer it correctly, you get twice the money. If you lose, you lose everything. Which will it be?"

"We'll try the question," said Robin with determination. His voice cracked ever so slightly as he spoke, but this time there were no titters from the audience. They were far too interested. Actually, his words surprised him when he heard them, but the girl smiled approvingly. She's dead game all the way, he thought. That's a lot of money. For me it's the difference between hiking home or taking a plane or a train.

"Very good then. Here's the Stickler. You have fifteen seconds in which to answer. Ready? Here it is."

He hesitated a moment, glanced down at the notes in his hand. Silence descended, and Robin felt the same uneasy tension in the air as when he stood poised at the end of the runway, pole in his hands, waiting for the last try. When a whole track meet and the failure or success of an entire season hung on his clearing that bar. When the faces of the throng around the pit were blurred, just as the faces of those people beyond the footlights were indistinct. When everything depended upon one chance.

"Here's the question," said Whiskers, pausing. "Ready? Here's the question." He hesitated, waiting, making it as difficult for them as possible. "What is on the back of a Jefferson nickel?"

A Jefferson nickel? Why . . . a nickel . . . sure . . . a nickel . . . a Jefferson nickel . . . Come now, quick. I've seen hundreds of nickels. The back of a Jefferson nickel! The front . . . the back . . . and never noticed . . . never noticed the back.

The silence grew, increased, hung over them like a storm. No one spoke, nobody moved. Here goes our four hundred, that's for sure. He saw Whiskers' relentless eyes fixed on the second hand of his watch. The man's arm went up in the air.

"Monticello," said the girl quietly, as if she had been teaching a history class in school.

"*Right!*" shouted Whiskers. "Right! The eight hundred is yours, and a bonus of another hundred for answering all the questions. Monticello is correct. The student and the teacher . . . win nine hundred dollars . . . with the compliments . . ."

His words were lost. The noise was terrific. Beside Robin the girl was dancing up and down. She turned and, throwing her arms around him, kissed his cheek. The crowd loved it. So, too, did Robin.

Chapter 17

"LET'S celebrate. Why don't we go out on the town?" Bob was not quite sure what this meant, but it made him feel like a man of the world. "It's my last night here. Why don't we go out and celebrate?" He touched his inside pocket, where a check for four hundred and fifty dollars reposed.

They were driving through the usual maze of Los Angeles traffic, a confusion of signs, lights, and cars all going fifty-five or better.

To his surprise, she shook her head with decision. "Nothing doing. I'm not letting you spend that money. We'll go to my little place in Pasadena. It costs a lot of money to go anywhere in L.A. I need that cash. If you're a student you need it too. Now you won't have to hitchhike home, for one thing."

"But look, I could get a ticket to New York on a jet plane and still have enough left to buy you a beer." Once again, he felt very old and worldly. "C'mon, please."

"No, thanks. You use the money for something worth while."

He suddenly wondered whether he should change his plans about leaving town the next day. After all, it makes a difference when you know people, when you have friends in a town. "I never went to a big broadcast like this before," he said. "You know you were really hot out there. You were on top of things all the way; you pulled me through. Believe me, I was plenty scared at first before all those people."

She patted his knee with her right hand. He liked it. "You didn't seem a bit scared, the way you gave it back to Tommy Dunn. What's more, I certainly couldn't help you with the question about the horse's teeth."

"Oh . . . that! I guessed that."

"And I just guessed Monticello!"

They both laughed happily. The strain was over and it was easy to be gay. She swung her little coupé into a six-lane boulevard down which cars pounded at fearful speed. No more standing there with an arm out. No more nights alone under bridges. He was exhilarated by the change in his fortunes, by the amazingly attractive girl beside him, even by the automobiles that overtook them and whizzed past.

"Just where is that . . . Five Mile River? Is that a real name?"

"Of course. It's about fifty miles from New York, in Connecticut."

"I see. And you go to Yale. I better confess that I've always wanted to meet a Yale man. Yes, I really have." He could see she was impressed. Once again he realized how different was his feeling about Yale out here from the way he felt at home.

"Why?" he asked.

"Oh . . . I don't know. The boys from the East . . . they have something. I can't explain." She sighed a little. "You're a pole vaulter, aren't you? I know a boy at Southern Cal who's a pole vaulter, on the track team. Used to be a high jumper, too, but he gave that up."

Bob responded immediately. "Pole vaulters are usually all-round athletes. But golf is really my game. I love golf better than anything. I'd rather shoot a game of golf than eat."

"Good for you. I love golf, too. We have some pretty fair golfers out here: Dave Johnson, Sonny Proctor. He was finalist in the Amateur last year at Merion."

"I know," said Bob hastily. "Maybe if I stayed over we could have a game. Do you think so?"

"Why, I'd enjoy it a lot. Look, you've only just got to Los Angeles; you haven't seen the place. Why d'you have to leave?"

This brought him up against facts. There were still ten days in August left, and now that he had money to fly East he could stay a week or more and still reach home before the first of September. Certainly it would be fun to stay a few more days, with some friends in the place.

The little coupé buzzed into Pasadena, turned down a side street, went round a corner, and drew up at her front door. There was no light in the house, and they went onto the porch while she fumbled in her purse for the key. Just as she put it in the lock they could both hear the telephone ringing inside. She let him in and turned on the lights. It was a two-story house, and with a teacher friend she occupied the ground floor.

"Everyone and his dog will be calling me now. That Tommy Dunn show is the most popular thing on the air," she said. Yet she didn't hurry especially, and by the time she had turned on the light and reached the telephone, it had stopped ringing. "Oh, never mind. They'll ring again. Would you like something to eat?"

"Great, I'm hungry. I'd like anything you got." She left him, went into the kitchen, and he heard drawers open, a refrigerator door shut with a bang. It made things seem intimate and homelike.

Between that moment and the time she finally came out of the kitchen with a tray of sandwiches, salad, and coffee, the telephone rang half a dozen times. At first he listened to her conversations with amusement, heard the congratulations and the comments, and enjoyed her rejoinders. Especially when she said, "That's right, Louise. I always did want to meet a Yale man." She flashed that smile across the room at him, her eyebrows raised slightly. "Uh-huh. Yes, he is. He's nicer than that."

After a few more calls he began to feel somewhat out of things. One after another, boys and girls kept calling, for apparently, as she had predicted, everybody in Los Angeles had been listening that evening to the Tommy Dunn hour. At last the two sat down together to the tray, but before she had finished one sandwich, the telephone rang again. She rose, the sandwich in her hand, munching between sentences. When finally she turned back, he had one of her schoolbooks in his hand and she noticed it.

"Look," she said, "I have something to confess."

"What?" He was astonished. "What's that?"

"I'm not really a teacher. I mean I'm not a real teacher . . . yet. I'm studying in the City College and doing substitute training at Long Beach."

He threw back his head and laughed. "Great! That's fine. Because I'm not at Yale, either."

Her face fell. "You're not?"

"No, but I'm supposed to go next year."

The telephone jangled again. "What a nuisance!" said the girl, somewhat impatiently. "Shall I let it ring?"

"Why not? Let it ring."

But conversation is not easy in the face of a jangling, noisy telephone. Moreover, the person on the other end was insistent. Instead of giving up shortly, the ringing persisted. Surely somebody was determined to get her, even if it was necessary to ring all night.

At last she gave in, rose, and took up the receiver. Her tone, however, had annoyance in it as she answered. "Yes . . . yes, it is. Yes, this is Maryjanehayes. I say, this is Miss Hayes speaking. Who? Why, no, I'm sorry. There's no Robin here . . ."

He jumped. Ten minutes before he had been a Yale man, a track star at New Haven, who went out on the town at night. Now, hang it all, his family were trailing him down. It was humiliating. How on earth, he wondered as he grabbed the telephone, had they ever managed to locate him here in Pasadena?

"Yes?"

He heard his father's familiar tone. "That you, Robin old boy?"

"Hey there, hello, Dad! How are you?" Despite his annoyance, it was good to talk to him again.

"Well, well, congratulations! We had to call to congratulate you. Your mother and I got most of your broadcast and we *loved* it. You held your own with that chap, Robin, and a good deal more. I was proud of you. I was mighty glad to hear you hand it back to him about Yale."

"Gee, thanks, Dad. But Miss Hayes really pulled me through."

"Why, no such thing; you pulled yourself through. Couldn't have been cooler if you'd been a radio veteran." This pleased Robin; he was especially glad they had missed the beginning of the broadcast. "Now, son, when are you planning to come home? This place here is pretty quiet without you; it's getting lonesome."

"Yes, Dad. But there are several things here I

hafta do. Might be a day or so yet. 'Course now I'll come by train or air. Say, Dad, tell me how you knew I was here?"

His father's warm and agreeable laugh sounded in his ear. "Well, your mother said if you were my son you'd probably be somewhere with that girl. We remembered her name, so we just called her number. Hold on a minute. Your mother wants to talk to you."

There was the merest pause. She must have been standing at his side.

"Oh, Robin, darling, you were *simply wonderful.* We were so proud of you. The Maxwells called and said you were on the program, and we got most of it. I do wish we'd heard it all. The way you stood up to that horrid man . . ."

"He was all right, Mother. That's his job . . . to needle people a little."

She paid no attention. "And gave all those answers. I told Dad I don't believe many boys would have given those answers like that."

"I had some help, Mother." He winked at the girl across the room, and she flashed her smile back at him.

"Nonsense. It was you who answered the questions. Now, Robin . . ."

"Bob, Mother."

Of course she paid no attention. She was far too excited. "Now, Robin darling, you'll come directly back, won't you? I'd much rather you took the train than the plane. And now hadn't you better get your sleep? If you're going to have that long train journey tomorrow?"

"*Mother!*" This was too much. "Thanks for calling, Mother. It was great to talk to you and Dad. G'by, Mother. See you soon. G'by."

He smacked the telephone down, hoping the girl had not heard all his mother's admonitions and suggestions. Mothers were really something. They just did not understand when a fellow was grown up.

Then to his surprise the girl walked over toward him and, taking the receiver, laid it gently on the table beside the stand. "There! Your people have called you, and just about everyone in L.A. has called me, and that's about enough. How about a little quiet for a while?" She took him by the arm and led him to the divan. "They want you to come right back to Connecticut, don't they, Bob? They think most likely you're in the arms of a siren or something?"

It was the first time she had called him by his name, his real name. This girl was so vital, so much more alive than the girls at home. Why, Pamela Griswold was insipid compared to her. He disliked the very thought of Pamela Griswold. She was a child. No girl had ever appealed to him before in quite this way. Surely he could stay a few days in California if he wished. Actually, if he took a plane he could remain almost a week and still reach home in plenty of time. He had made no promise; he hadn't said he would start back the next day.

There was a sudden stomping on the front porch. She rose, thinking it was her roommate. He rose too, listening. The footsteps went upstairs into the other apartment.

He knew he should be getting back to Los Angeles, yet he hated to leave. She came toward him and took hold of the lapels of his coat. "We could have that golf game if you stayed a day or two," she said.

Suddenly his legs felt weak and he trembled exactly as he had when he stumbled out into the lights of the stage earlier that evening. He turned and put his arms around her. I'm going to kiss her, he thought. Right now. I sure am.

Then her roommate returned.

It was twenty minutes later when he went down the steps to seek the only taxi stand in town which, they told him, was open all night. He bounded onto the pavement. Actually, it was not pavement, it was air on which he walked. This was what they sang about, this exhilaration, this marvelous feeling. He wanted to run, to leap into space. He had no fatigue at all, felt as fresh as at the start of a track meet. I could vault twenty feet now, he thought. There was no sense of weariness in him. So this was what they called love.

Chapter 18

HE uncorked himself and smacked the ball. *Zzzzoom* . . . it sailed far down the fairway. Mary Jane stood beside him, shading her eyes with her hand, watching his drive scream into the distance until she lost sight of it two hundred and fifty yards away.

"Wow! You're really a golfer! I had no idea you could hit a ball like that," she said as they walked off the tee. Her admiration was evident. "Can you vault as well as you play golf?"

He laughed with pleasure. "It's the air out here, I think." It really was, too. That queer, light feeling of exhilaration still possessed him. He felt he could run, jump, hit a ball, do anything better than he had ever done it before. No wonder, he realized, California turned out the best athletes in the nation.

This was the third day after the broadcast, and he had seen Mary Jane on each one of the three days. He waved his club at a blade of grass. "I sure love golf. Pole vaulting is chest exercises and arm exercises and leg exercises, and practice, practice, practice all the time."

"Oh, I wouldn't want to pole-vault. It's much too dangerous. Hanging up there fifteen feet in the air! No, thanks, not for me."

"Well . . . no, it really isn't dangerous, Mary Jane. I never had anything happen to me except a few ankle sprains, maybe. Then last spring in a track meet I had to run the high hurdles and pulled a cartilage in my knee. That laid me up the best part of six weeks."

"But doesn't it shake you all to pieces when you drop that far, when you come down?"

"Oh, no, it doesn't shake you, not if you know how to fall. A trained jumper usually lands on his feet; he knows how to relax when he hits the sawdust. You can break a pole, of course, but even then a jumper who knows his business doesn't get hurt. The drudgery is what I dislike. Pole vaulting is work. You've no idea how you have to stay with it. Chin-ups and pull-ups and hours and hours indoors on the horizontal bars, all that kind of thing. I began vaulting when I was nine or ten. Practice, practice, all the time. Fact is, I should have been practicing this week. I'd really like to get a workout some place."

"You would? Well, I tell you what. I'll get hold of Johnny Rogers for you. He'll be glad to give you a workout. Johnny vaults for Southern Cal. Remember? I spoke about him the other night. He's a marvelous athlete. Johnny's marvelous, period."

There was a tone in her voice, a kind of soft tone that Robin did not care for at all. He hastily told himself that he had imagined that sound which grated so unpleasantly on his ears.

"No, *thanks*. I'd rather work out alone. I wouldn't be able to give him any competition at all. I'm completely out of practice."

"Well, Johnny hasn't had much time to practice lately. He manages a filling station from noon until late at night. I'll have him call you at the Y. You'll like Johnny Rogers. Everyone does."

Sure enough, when he got back to his room at the Y. in Los Angeles, there was a message that Johnny Rogers would pick him up the next morning at nine.

Bob was downstairs and ready when a big fellow in a sports shirt and tan trousers, with a mass of blond hair, walked hurriedly across the lobby, searching for him. "Bob Longe? Glad to see you. I figured that was you." He stuck out an enormous fist.

"Yeah, glad to see you. Thanks for coming round. It's mighty good of you." They went out and climbed into Johnny's car, Bob actually feeling small beside this giant. "This is going to be a lot of fun. But I don't believe I'll be able to do much. I haven't touched a pole since I left home almost two months ago."

"That's right. Jenny told me you haven't had much chance to practice lately."

"Jenny?"

"Why, sure. Mary Jane, but everyone calls her Jenny." There was a possessive note here that Bob disliked, a familiar air that was unpleasant.

When they reached the Southern California gymnasium a little later, Bob instantly realized he was in the company of a celebrity. Everyone seemed to know him and everybody addressed him with respect.

"Hi, Johnny!"

"Hello there, Johnny-boy. Where you been keeping yourself all summer?"

"Hey, look who's here! How are you, Johnny?"

Clothes were brought and an outfit for Bob was selected. They rubbed some skin hardener on the palms of their hands. Then, taking four or five poles, they went into the warm sunshine and out to the track. To his amazement, Bob felt happy to have spiked shoes on once again. He danced up and down on the thick turf, a wonderful feeling.

"Say, this is great. This is sure pole-vaulting weather. Fella couldn't jump on a day like this, he wouldn't be much good. I don't suppose you get it like this every day, though."

"No," said the big boy, hefting one pole, then lifting up another, sighting along it, testing it in his hand. "No, but we can work out nearly every day we want to. That's why we beat records out in this country. The best pole vaulters come from California." This remark was not made boastfully but simply as a statement of fact, uttered in the most casual tones.

"I know," agreed Bob. "But the Yale crew beat California and Washington last spring." Not for the first time he realized that he was standing up for Yale.

The big chap, still hefting poles, remarked, "Yeah . . . we don't have a crew here." He sounded as if crew was inconsequential, like checkers or badminton. "But we have the best tennis players and golfers and we always win in track, because we can run and jump here the year round. Makes a big difference in a man's training."

Once again Bob had to agree. Weather like wine certainly did make a difference.

The Californian jogged a few feet down the grass, returned, and said, "Why do you want to go to Yale, anyhow? Why don't you come out here to school?"

"Well, fact is I've been thinking about it. Only thing is, my dad and his old man were both pole vaulters at Yale, and Dad sort of counts on my going there. You know, Yale has made a specialty of the pole vault and the coaching is wonderful. They go in for action pictures and that sort of thing. Pole vaulting is kind of a tradition at New Haven."

"I see. But here we practice the year round outdoors. Fella can't help improving. What good is tradition if you're not up around fourteen feet or more?"

This was hard to answer. "I know. I'd like to go to college out here." He trotted several yards down the cinder path, digging his spikes in and increasing his speed; then he slowed down and returned. Stretching out on the grass, he kicked his legs vigorously into the air. "This is sure great; it's wonderful."

He sat up as the big fellow stood poised at the end of the runway with a pole in his hand, started off, and suddenly put on a burst of speed. Bob watched enviously. The Californian was the ideal build for a pole vaulter, about six feet two, one hundred and eighty pounds of muscle. He fairly ate up the track, and speed, as Bob well knew, is one of the secrets of good vaulting. If you cannot generate speed on the runway, you jackknife or fall back. If you do that, you tumble onto the hard cinders of the path. And no one would forget that in a hurry.

Yes, this blond giant really had it. Compared with him, Bob felt about as thick as the pole he balanced tentatively in his hands.

Together they lay on their backs on the grass and did setting-up exercises; then they sprinted down the path, warming up slowly. Bob had an uneasy feeling as he watched this big man go about things in a brisk, businesslike manner. Once his father had told him that the trained athlete gets out, warms up, makes a quick inspection to see that everything is right, and then takes his pole and jumps. No fuss, no ceremony. Bob knew it was invariably the poorer athletes, the ones who dropped out the second time the bar was raised, who horsed around half an hour before being ready to jump.

Bob peeled off his sweater, went up to the bars, and paced off seventy feet on the path. He dropped his sweater there on the grass. This would be his second check point. His left foot must hit this point exactly if he was to leave the ground in proper stride. Then he walked farther back and laid down his handkerchief one hundred and twenty feet from the bar—his first mark. Finally he sprinted up and down, dashing under the bar and coming back several times.

He knew what he had to do: run as hard as he could, slide the pole into an unyielding eight-inch wooden slot, absorb the consequent shock, then hoist his hundred and fifty-five pounds skyward, feet first, over the bar, tossing the pole backward as he went.

"I'm ready," he said.

"Go ahead, Bob."

"No, you go ahead. You're home team."

The big fellow's spikes grated and scratched the cinder path with that old, familiar noise. He was off like a locomotive. His body rose, arched gracefully up and out, the pole clattered to the cinder path, and one saw blue sky between the body and the bar. The whole performance was effortless.

Bob rose, dancing on his toes. You're on the spot now, he thought. Better make this good.

He leaned forward with a frown on his face, concentrating. Then he started slowly, gathered speed, hit both check marks exactly, felt the familiar unpleasant shock as the pole hit the slot, and was cleanly over the crossbar, dropping to the dirt below. It was hard not to feel pleased, for he knew his form had been perfect.

The big chap took his jump calmly, saying nothing. Together they balanced the bar and raised it up.

"What is it now?"

"Only twelve-six."

Only twelve-six. Bob lay down on his back, kicked his legs in the air, rolled over and over in the grass to loosen up. Then he rose and looked at the bar. Thirteen feet, he knew, was a winning jump in intercollegiate track meets. He was in the big time now.

The Californian, pole in hand, stood scowling at the bar as he made ready for his next try. Suddenly he leaped forward, turned on that fantastic speed, hit the cinders like a hundred-yard-dash man, rose into the air with the agility of an acrobat, went up . . . up . . . up and over.

"Good work. Attaboy!" said Bob, trying to make his words sound enthusiastic. But his tone was flat and he knew it.

Bob needed a couple of tries this time, only just

managing to get over the bar, which jiggled but stayed on. At twelve-eight, the Californian hit the bar and again it stayed in place. Once more Bob had to jump twice to get over. He came back shaking his head, murmuring, "I'm out of practice. I haven't got the feel of things." The second the words were out, he hated himself. It was one of Dad's beliefs that the good athlete never apologizes for a bad showing and never excuses himself. He simply tries harder and does better the next time.

Twelve-ten, and they both squeezed over. This was the highest Bob had ever reached. Yet somehow in that summer sunshine, under the stress of competition again, he felt his keenness returning, his confidence coming back.

For the first time the Californian jiggled the bar ever so slightly and it tumbled to the ground. "Shoot! That's plain careless. Go ahead, Bob, go on."

Unlimbering his legs, Bob squatted a few times, then gripped his pole and stood motionless, summoning every bit of will power for the seconds to come. In a good vault everything must go right. One difficulty is that you have it all there before you every second as you go down the runway. He leaned over, trying to remember his coaching, darted forward, gathered speed, hit the slot perfectly, went up and around, shoving the pole backward. As he arched out he knew it was a perfect jump. From

the sawdust below there was that gorgeous sight—
the crossbar still on the uprights.

"Great stuff! Say, fella, you can jump. I bet you've
been coached by Californians. No? Well, I'll hand
it you. The Yales turn out jumpers, don't they? O.K.
No funny business. Here goes!"

He was off, rising like a great eagle, clearing the
bar gracefully and easily, landing on his feet and
rolling deftly onto his left side.

"Let's go up to thirteen," he said.

Bob turned away, because to him thirteen feet was
a lot of jumping. Here's where I get the works;
here's where I'm shown up, he thought. He lay on
his back, kicked his legs in the air, brought them up
over his head a dozen times. Hang it, this guy is
Superman. I really believe Tommy Dunn was right;
if a kid can't do the hundred in ten flat when he's
born, they chuck him back into the Pacific Ocean.

The big chap trotted over, shaking his great mass
of hair. He removed his sweat shirt, anything but a
reassuring gesture. "Yeah, that's better. I did fourteen in a dual meet with Stanford, but the officials
checked, and darned if they didn't find the bar was
on the wrong peg."

"Did you ever run the hundred?"

"Yep. I did nine-seven once."

Bob gasped. The Yale record was nine-seven.
"How 'bout the quarter?"

"Oh, the quarter. I haven't run the quarter since freshman year. Did forty-seven-six then."

Again Bob gasped at the casual statement. The Yale record for the quarter was forty-eight seconds. This big guy really had it. He rose, trying once more to ignore the height of the bar. Here, somehow, he felt he represented Yale. It was a kind of contest, and there was responsibility on him. Then a phrase of Dad's came to him, something about sending a boy to do a man's work. He was the boy; this Superman was the adult.

He also recalled something else. It was a warm, sunny spring afternoon in a track meet with Choate. Jimmy Fitz, Taft's best sprinter, was out with a Charley horse; and Tim Byrnes, the hurdler and captain, was laid up in the infirmary with an attack of the flu. Consequently they were outclassed, beaten before they began.

Before the meet Bob had asked the coach for permission to try the hundred and the broad jump, as well as the pole vault. The coach agreed and he took seconds in the first two, and won the high jump. So the two teams came down to the last event, tied in the point score.

The crowd had gathered about the pit, speechless, while each man took his turn. The sun sank lower; a damp chill came up off the lake. Bob was bushed. He had nothing left after the long day of competition, unlike Tony Briggs of Choate, who was fresh and keen. Yet somehow he had to get up and over that bar. Somehow he did, too, summoning hidden reserves as they pushed it up, until he finally won at twelve-ten. It was Tony who failed on the third try.

The one-man track team, they had called him at the Alumni Dinner that night. Hadn't he won eighteen points alone, and practically pulled the team through all by himself? Yet it was not that he remembered, or the crowd around him afterward in the lockers, or the cups he lugged to his room.

Dad had sat next to him at dinner, taking these triumphs calmly and casually. What Bob remembered now in this moment of crisis was a remark Dad had made in even tones to the headmaster. "Bob's a good athlete; the good athlete always rises to the big moment. That's the difference between just a fine player and a star."

That was Dad twenty-five years before, too; Dad in the Intercollegiates beating the Californians, or jumping in the Olympics against Bull, the Norwegian champion. It was Hogan, the golfer, besting the field in the Open after a terrible automobile crash had crippled him; it was . . .

"You're up, fella."

He was back in the California sunshine. Slowly he rose, leaning over for his pole. He stood on his toes, concentrating with everything he had. Making those extra inches was, he knew, a matter of the sprint.

Can you turn it on? Can you run fifty yards at top speed and resist the shock when the pole hits the box?

"Wait a minute. Hold on, Bob. Mind if I make a suggestion?"

He turned, swinging the pole around. "I should say not. I'd be glad for any help at all."

"Well, this may be all wrong. You know your sprint better'n I do. But I believe, since you haven't got a lot of beef, you'd get more speed and more power if you'd start five yards farther back. I know I can generate speed in a shorter distance than some of the other fellows on the team. It's just a suggestion. . . ."

It sounded intelligent. He knew he did lack the power of the big Californian. "I'll try it. No harm giving it a try." So he paced off five yards, got the exact starting line for his stride, and stood holding the pole. Then he got moving, gathered speed, but failed to hit his first check mark correctly. So he raced under the bar, turned, and trotted slowly back again.

Sitting down, he kicked his legs in the air, trying to relax. His hands were tender from disuse, and now there were bloody calluses on the palms. He hardly noticed them. He rose, measured his check marks carefully, wound the tape on the pole so it wouldn't cut his hands, flexed his knees, and stood on his toes. The real athlete rises to the occasion. This is it.

Once more he raced down the runway, hit his marks, struck the box, and pulled up with all his force . . . hung there . . . over . . . and dropped below. The bar was still in place. Sawdust was in his eyes, sawdust was in his hair, sawdust was in his nose and ears and up his pants. He didn't care. Hey, I'm higher than I've ever been before, higher than I hoped to get this year. I showed the big guy. I did a man's job.

"Great guns!" said the Californian, sitting up. There was admiration in his voice now. "That's jumping, kid. You were three inches over that bar then, d'you know that? You really got it, fella."

They went on for ten minutes. Johnny cleared thirteen-two; Bob failed. But he had done better than his best when he had to, so this did not bother him. He was content when the Californian said, "That's plenty for me. Tell you what, Bob. I'm going to speak to Jack Hathaway about you. He's director of athletics here at school. We need fellows like you at Southern Cal."

Chapter 19

"LET me have that seven iron, boy."

The tone sounded abrupt, and most certainly he had not intended to use that tone. Now, he realized, he was talking exactly like a dozen men he had caddied for across the country. They had snapped at him in just that way. Funny what a difference being on the other side of the fence did make. Well, I probably wouldn't even have realized this two months ago, he reflected.

The caddie, leaning on his golf bag, was only a year or so Bob's junior. "Most of the men players need a five iron to hit that green from here," he remarked cautiously.

"Yeah, but I'd like to try my seven, just for the fun of it, and see what I can do."

He took the club the caddie handed him and sighted the green in the far distance, a long seven-iron shot. Immediately he wished he had taken the caddie's advice. Caddies, he realized, usually know far more about distances and courses than players do. That's a long, long swipe. Well, too late now.

This better be good, or else. Or else I'll know exactly what that kid behind me is thinking.

Taking plenty of time, he flexed his knees, relaxed, and wiggled the club. Then he took a full, easy swing and felt that wonderful sensation of perfect connection between club and ball. When he looked up, the little white thing was barely visible, scudding along the entrance to the green between the traps, stopping close up to the flag.

"Golly!" said the boy. "They isn't many members could pull that one off with a seven iron."

It's the air, Bob felt, it's the air. I just can't miss. This place has everything.

That shot gave him a birdie on the hole and he birdied the next hole, too. All his strokes went exactly right; his drives sailed straight down the middle of the fairway, his putts sank. It was a gorgeous feeling.

All at once his mind reverted to the Junior Championships at Oakland Hills in Detroit, which were due to begin soon. Playing this kind of a game, he could make trouble for anybody, he felt sure. I'd certainly like to take a crack at that tournament, he thought. So he pulled out his purse and checked on a small calendar he carried. The pro had said the tournament began on the twenty-eighth. Why, that's tomorrow! Impossible. Anyway, it's much more important to stay right here. So he went on and finished the round, completely relaxed. His score was a thirty-eight, the lowest he had ever made.

It had been a long day, starting early in the morning when Johnny called at the Y., stacked his luggage in the car, and drove him out to the Southern California campus. He met a dozen people and finally was taken into the office of Mr. Hathaway, the director of athletics.

Never had Bob met such friendly people, so anxious to help, as these agreeable Californians. It appeared that with his College Boards behind him, he could enter the university without any examinations. Moreover, an athletic scholarship that would take care of his tuition and his room rent was mentioned. They helped him fill out his application blanks, explaining what he needed in the way of transcripts from school.

Now all he had to do was sell Dad that he wasn't going to Yale!

Johnny dropped him at a hotel in Pasadena, for Bob wanted to be nearer Mary Jane during the last days of his visit. After a late lunch, he had played that round of golf on the municipal course, enjoying the luxury of having a caddie instead of caddying for himself or for someone else. The first thing he did on returning to the hotel was to write a long letter to his father, explaining that he was coming home the end of the week by air and that he was considering a year at Southern California. It seemed wiser to break the news now, to allow them a few days to get over the shock instead of surprising them suddenly on his arrival.

After finishing the letter, he started to prepare for his evening date. A bellhop brought back his flannel trousers, newly pressed, and the blue blazer with the red shield over the breast pocket. He had bought a razor and, although he really didn't need it, he decided to shave. Then he put on his best pink shirt with the buttoned collar and the striped school necktie. Looking at himself in the mirror, he was satisfied.

After a shine in the hotel basement, he felt he had done his best and was ready. He posted his letter and glanced at the clock in the lobby, which said five-thirty. He was not due at Mary Jane's house, four blocks away, until six. There was an eternity to kill.

Buying a newspaper, he sat down to the sports pages and an account of the feverish pennant race in the National League. The Dodgers were always like that, always hanging on somehow. In the Pacific Coast League the Angels were winning the title, and it took him several minutes to realize that the Angels were Los Angeles. When he looked again at the clock, it was only twenty-one minutes of six.

Thrusting aside the paper, he went into the florist shop next door and bought two dozen red roses. The roses were like everything in California, the biggest and best he had ever seen. Also they were expensive.

But money was to spend, after all, especially when you had made it yourself.

With the roses under his arm, he started out in the setting sun, walking around three extra blocks, trying to kill the unmoving moments until he could be with her again. At last he came down her street, walking slowly, as slowly as he could, toward her house. This was living. Never had he felt so keen, so excited, so alive.

When he reached the porch, his foot on the top step, he heard her voice through the open window. Evidently she was talking on the telephone. "But, Johnny-dear . . ."

He recognized that same deep, warm, affectionate tone which he had so disliked when she told him about Johnny Rogers. Fear struck him. It was a new kind of fear, a fear he had never felt before. He stood motionless as she went on talking.

"But, darling, you're making something out of nothing. He's just a kid. He's a sweet kid and he doesn't know a soul here. . . . Why, he'd never think of such a thing. I could be his grandmother."

The fear spread, increased, bewildered him, made him suddenly dizzy, took possession of his senses.

"Well, I don't want him to be hurt, either. You're just making too much of it. . . . Oh, all right." Now her tone was slightly annoyed. "All *right*. I'll tell him this evening . . . I say I'll tell him we're engaged. . . . All right, silly. Of course I do, Johnny. You know I do."

Bob turned down the steps and walked away. It was the same pavement which had been liquid air only a few nights before. A few nights—yet years, centuries ago.

Everything around seemed the same, yet nothing was the same. He felt completely and utterly changed. People walked past, the setting sun still shone, cars went down the street. But a moment of time had dissolved his whole world in misery.

Why hadn't he realized it the moment Johnny Rogers spoke of her in that possessive way when they were pole-vaulting? Why . . . why . . . why . . . why hadn't he known that love was like this? That it could make you ache all over with pain, an unendurable pain. That it could stun you into dizziness, so you didn't know what you were doing. Why, I never knew that love could *hurt* like this.

The hotel suddenly loomed up before him. He started across the street. A car honked angrily and he saw he was going against the lights. No matter, he ducked over anyway. He didn't care what happened. Plunging into the lobby, he went directly to the transportation desk. "I've got to be in Detroit tomorrow morning. How soon could you get me out by plane?"

The man looked up, surprised. He thought a moment. "Let me see now. There's a fast flight on

TWA for Chicago, and you could change for Detroit at Chicago. That is, if you're about ready to leave for the airport. Are you all set to go if I can get the reservation?" He held the telephone, looking at Bob.

"Sooner the better. That suits me. In ten minutes I'll be packed and settle the bill. You get a cab and have it waiting outside."

He turned quickly toward the elevator, then suddenly turned back again to the man behind the desk. "Here, take these." He pushed an armful of roses into the clerk's astonished hands.

Chapter 20

"ON the tee! On the tee! Jimmy Johnston. Robert B. Longe."

One boy stood alone on the tee, swinging his driver carelessly with one hand, waiting while the officials called out to each other or addressed the group standing around.

"Robert B. Longe. L-o-n-g-e. Longe, with an *E*. Has he checked in yet? No? Why don't they get here when they're called? The starting times were all published this morning."

"Longe hasn't shown yet. If it's his starting time, better default him," someone called out.

"Well, we certainly can't hold the other matches. If he isn't here . . . that's his lookout."

"Hey, wait a minute!" a voice shouted from the clubhouse. "Longe is here; just came in by taxi."

Seconds later Bob pushed through the crowd, dressed in his blue Taft blazer and flannel trousers, his golf bag over his shoulder, and stepped up to the officials with clip boards and pencils in their hands.

"Sorry if I'm late, sir! I only reached the airport

at eight. My connection from the Coast was an hour late getting into Chicago. Then it seemed to take me all morning to get out here."

"You Longe, Robert B. Longe? Well, son, you're sure cutting things fine. We were just going to default you. Glad we didn't have to, glad you made it. We hate to scratch anyone. All right now. Caddies! On the tee—Jimmy Johnston of Lakeland, Florida, and Robert B. Longe of Five Mile River, Connecticut!"

Bob had spent a sleepless night on the plane, tortured and unhappy every moment. There was reason enough not to play well, plenty of excuses for being off his game. But he knew perfectly well that excuses don't matter. The only thing that matters in golf is to play the ball as it lies. The only thing that counts is the final score.

The previous day on the municipal course at Pasadena . . . was it only a few hours or was it a few years back? . . . everything had gone right. Today on the rolling fairways and well-trapped greens of Oakland Hills, everything went wrong. He found every bunker, was off course much of the way. Luckily his adversary, a lanky youth of about fifteen, had a bad case of tournament fever. In a word, he was frightened. Only this saved Bob in that morning match.

His afternoon opponent was a cocky youngster with freckles, who seemed to be a favorite in the locker room. Everybody knew him, for he had been out practicing on the course for three days, and he was addressed as Sandy by young and old. With young and old he joked, laughed, and kidded. Bob guessed his age at about twelve. He hardly seemed a dangerous threat, which was a relief.

"You say you hitchhiked all the way from Baltimore alone?" an older man said.

"Sure, why not?" There was complete assurance in the youngster's reply.

"Aren't you a little young to be hitchhiking from Baltimore to Detroit?" the man asked.

"Oh, I get around," said the youngster, with complete self-possession.

He carried that attitude and poise onto the course. Within a couple of holes, Bob realized that the boy was no pushover. His shots, though seldom long, were straight. Although he did nothing very brilliant, he was never in trouble, either, keeping down the middle on each hole. He did not three-putt the greens, as Bob did once or twice. At the end of the first nine, the youngster was one up.

To be licked the first day by this freckled-faced kid —why, that's terrible, Bob thought, as he leaned over to tee up his ball on the tenth hole. His drive was long, and after a good approach and two putts he evened the score. He went ahead on the next hole, was pulled back on the twelfth, and lost the lead again on the thirteenth. They split the fourteenth and a crowd began to gather, for this was anyone's match.

On the fifteenth Bob hooked his drive into a clump of trees and was fortunate, thanks to a fine approach, to be on the green in three and to split the hole. He was still one down. The youngster was sailing along, as loose and unconcerned as if he were shooting a game for fun at his home club.

The sixteenth was the famous water hole. The boy smacked a wicked low drive down the fairway, and Bob followed with another straight one that was several yards longer. One glance told Bob that the second shots had to clear a pond, light on that guarded green, and stick. There was no room up there to fool around; one slip, and you were either in the traps or in the water.

The youngster's second was a real beauty, sailing diagonally over the pond, bounding along with little hops until it came to rest six feet from the hole. The gallery clapped. The boy thrust his iron back into the bag with a kind of swagger that said, Let's see you beat that shot. Shucks, that's nothing! I do that every day, the set of his shoulders seemed to say.

Bob stepped quickly up to his ball. He knew perfectly well what he had to do. Then he stopped and looked up in the act of addressing the ball. Like a flash, the picture of Sammy Gorman at Skokie came back to him. He remembered how the champion had taken time over every shot, over the shortest of putts and the simplest and easiest approach. That's my trouble today, he suddenly realized. I've been rushing the ball. Slow down, fella. Now or never; slow down. Take your time, take time on this shot especially.

Calmly he turned and walked over to his caddie, replaced the seven iron in his bag, fumbled around a minute carefully, then drew it out again. The seven was his favorite club. This shot certainly needed the best he had.

Turning, he went back slowly toward the ball, sighting the green ahead, studying the flag and the slope of the ground around and above it. Now, now then! This is it! I have to make it this time. Only one chance. I must.

He drew back slowly, brought the club down, holding his head down as his body swung through, just as Gorman had done at Skokie. A ripple, a murmur from the scattered group around the green yanked him out of his concentration.

The ball fell, smacking the grass twenty feet above the cup, and rolled ever so gently and surely back down toward the flag. It died four feet away, an easy chance for a birdie three.

Now the pressure was the other way. The boy did not enjoy it, either; that was plain. He swaggered across to his caddie, took the proffered putter, and stepped up. Addressing the ball, he hit it quickly. It rolled down, struck the rim of the cup, bounced on, and stopped two feet away.

There, that's it, thought Bob. He's rattled. I know; I've seen it dozens of times in track meets. A guy holds on and holds on and then, *bang,* something happens and he cracks. That's enough to rattle anyone. He had me cold and now he isn't so sure. I jarred him when he felt he had the match in the bag, by getting inside him on this green. Then that putt—that was really bad luck. Well, here's the big one. Hit it, hit it firmly. Don't stab at it. Hit it cleanly.

The ball rolled gently down and plopped into the cup. The match was even. Bob never lost another hole and the boy went down on both seventeenth and eighteenth. On the final green, the youngster gave Bob a hurried handshake and turned away, tears in his eyes.

Bob looked over the menu with care. Breakfast on the morning of an important match is not an unimportant matter.

"Bacon and eggs . . . plenty of toast . . . lots of toast, please . . . double orange juice . . ."

"Double orange juice?" said the waitress.

"Yes'm, and two glasses of milk." He tossed the

menu down and quickly grabbed the morning paper in front of his plate.

"My, you're hungry today," said the waitress, flipping the menu under her arm as she turned away.

"Sure am," he replied, head buried in the paper. He turned eagerly to the sports pages to see whether the interview of the previous evening with a Detroit reporter was in this paper. One glance told him the story was merely an account of the day's play.

Robert B. Longe, Third, of Five Mile River, Connecticut, son of the old Yale track captain and Olympic star, reached the finals of the Junior Championships at the Oakland Hills Country Club yesterday, with a runaway eight-and-six victory over Sandy Lucas, former caddie, of Westfield, New Jersey. This morning Longe faces Dick Chandler of Red Wing, Minnesota, who beat Charley Morris, of Cincinnati, a high-school basketball star, three and two.

Young Longe, captain of his school track team and a third-generation pole vaulter, who attends Taft School in Connecticut, has been the sensation of the tournament. However, it seems unlikely he can beat Chandler, a sixteen-year-old high-school senior who reached the semifinals of the Amateur this year, and carries too many guns. But the pros around the course predict a greater future for Longe if he sticks to the game. It appears that Yale should have a golf star as well as a pole vaulter next year. The winner today receives a thousand-dollar scholarship to attend the college of his choice, the runner-up a five-hundred-dollar one. The match, which starts at ten this morning, will be for thirty-six holes.

Holy smoke, I'd forgotten all about those scholarships, Bob thought. Five hundred bucks! That's a lot of money. Now I can go to Southern Cal without costing Dad a cent. That is, if I really want to.

A familiar voice interrupted his thoughts. "It's bad luck to read your clippings the morning of a match, Robin!"

"Dad!" He jumped up. The early breakfasters in the Red Room of the Statler were astonished to see the tall, tanned boy embrace the older man and kiss him right there in public.

"Why, of course, of course I came." They were eating their breakfast together now, Bob thinking how wonderful it would be to have Dad in the gallery behind him, to have someone you loved near you, after days and days of being alone. This business of being on your own was all right, certainly was; only there comes a time when you need a person you trust close at hand. With Dad along, he couldn't help playing well. He would just have to win.

Soon they were riding out in the bus which took all the players, the officials, and the reporters to Oakland Hills, almost twenty-five miles from the city. Dad explained he had seen in an evening paper on his way to the station the results of the semifinals, so he returned to his office, grabbed an overnight bag he kept there, telephoned home, and caught the Detroiter at Grand Central. Quite by accident he had come to the Statler for breakfast.

"Yes, your mother is fine. She's certainly happy you're coming home again. Naturally she's been worried off and on all summer. I kept telling her that you were old enough to handle yourself in a broken field. But you know how women are . . . Oh, yes, Pamela Griswold called. She wanted to know just when you'd be back. Said you hadn't written lately."

He chatted as they sped through the suburbs, into rolling countryside, and finally reached the club before Bob had a chance to mention Yale or Southern Cal, either. He was just as glad to let things slide for the moment.

Slowly Bob dressed, surrounded by players, caddies, and the usual circle of older men. Before long the familiar call came from the loud-speaker on the wall. "On the tee. On the tee . . ."

Bob walked over to his locker and swung open the door. The locker was empty. "My clubs! My bag!" he gasped.

"Your clubs? Aren't they in the locker?" Dad took him by the arm.

A horrible thought assailed Bob. He tried to think back, slowly, carefully, calmly. This was no time to panic, this was the time to think things through.

He distinctly recalled taking the bag from his caddie and leaning it against one side of the locker.
Then came that interview with the sports writer as he
finished dressing. Next, suddenly, the last call for
the bus to town. He remembered slamming his
locker, turning with the reporter, and racing for
the bus. The clubs must have been left outside.

The attendant hurried up. Yes, he had seen them
leaning against the locker; thought they might belong to one of the members. A few minutes later he
had noticed they were gone but had paid no attention.

Hastily other lockers up and down the row were
opened. Every bag was hauled out and inspected with
attention; the whole room, the whole clubhouse was
searched.

"On the tee . . ." boomed the loud-speaker.
"Richard Chandler of Red Wing, Minnesota . . .
Robert B. Longe, Third, of Five Mile River, Con-
necticut."

"Hold it," someone shouted. "Tell them to hold
it on the tee a minute. Longe has lost his clubs. Hold
that out there, please."

The search became more frantic as minutes passed.

"Here, take mine. They're new . . ."

"What are yours, Wilson clubs? Use mine . . ."

"You can have my bag if you want . . ."

Offers came from every side. Naturally, he wanted
his own. Not only that he was used to them: to his

faithful old seven iron, chipped and scarred; to that beautiful four wood with the whip that sent the ball singing out low and straight on the fairway; to the ancient putter Dad had given him when he first started. It was more than golf clubs he had lost. They were old friends, companions who had been through good times with him and plenty of bad ones, too.

"Gee, Dad, I lugged that bag clean across the country. I'd rather lose that scholarship today than lose my clubs." His face was disconsolate.

His father hauled him into a corner. "Look, son, you're going to have to play with borrowed clubs. That's plain. Don't think about those clubs now. Don't let this upset you. Just go out there and play your game, win or lose. Yes, I know . . . I know . . . I know exactly how you feel, Robin. But don't let it get you down. Just go out there and hit that ball the best you can."

Bob walked grimly to the tee, his caddie following with the borrowed clubs. Whipping a driver back and forth stood a big chap about six feet two, with the shoulders of a boxer, who must have weighed a hundred and ninety pounds. He wore corrective bands on his teeth, which gave him a curiously youthful look. But, as they shook hands, Bob had no illusions. The guy was good.

"I'm Dick Chandler," he said pleasantly. "Sorry

to hear your clubs were stolen. That's a bad break for you."

Bob tried to smile, but it was a poor attempt. The referee was giving them their instructions. Out of bounds meant . . . that ditch on the third . . . the fourteenth was . . .

Bob hardly heard, hardly knew what the man was saying.

At first he dug in and tried hard to forget the loss of his clubs. Somehow he managed to hold on, although Chandler was outdriving him from ten to twenty yards off every tee. Luck, too, seemed to be with the big fellow. On the fifth he hit a booming drive into some woods. The ball hit a tree and caromed off far ahead up the fairway.

"Ah . . ." came a gasp from the gallery. They wanted Bob, the underdog, to win.

Yet slowly, surely, under the pressure from the other player, he felt himself slipping. A hole, another hole. Bob wanted desperately to win, with Dad there watching and rooting for him, Dad, who knew sports so well, who must have realized the hopelessness of it from the start.

After lunch the first nine going out was a nightmare. Bob simply went to pieces; his game disintegrated. He three-putted four greens and even had trouble with his short game. In his heart he knew it was not the clubs, unfamiliar though they were.

The fault was in himself. The trouble was in his game, which was not soundly built.

Now he saw plainly that it was easy to play record golf on the municipal course at Pasadena when there was no pressure, when a critical crowd was not watching your choice of each club, your swing on each shot. Then golf was a vastly different thing.

Good golf, he suddenly realized, like good pole vaulting or anything else, demands lots and lots of hard work, and lots and lots of practice.

Chapter 21

BOB and his father were seated beside each other in the plane bound for New York. It had helped to have Dad around the previous night. He did not say much. He had taken Bob to a movie and talked about other things than golf. Indeed there was not much you could say after a licking like that. But Dad was an athlete; he knew how you felt. Yes, it helped to have someone near you who understood what you were enduring.

Dad reached over and laid a hand on his arm. "Look, Robin, fella . . ."

"Bob, please, Dad."

"What's that? What d'you say?"

"Bob. The guys on the road this summer all called me Bob."

"Oh, I see. Of course. Well, Bob, I didn't say too much last night, but I want to tell you here and now I was proud of you."

"Proud! With a score like that? After that exhibition, after I blew up yesterday?" It all came pouring out.

"Wait a minute, my boy. You were up against a real golfer; that big fellow is hot stuff. He knows the game. After all, he was in the semifinals of the Amateur, wasn't he? Well, come now, wasn't he? Furthermore, he'd been playing in competition. This was his fifth straight tournament. He was tough; you know how much that means."

"Oh, yes, Dad, but to collapse that way, to go to pieces . . ."

"Now hold on. If some kid who had only polevaulted a couple of years tried to take you on in the Intercollegiate at New Haven, wouldn't you expect to beat him?"

"Why, yes, I suppose I would. Only . . ."

"Be reasonable, son. I tell you I was proud of you yesterday afternoon and I mean it, because what really counts is how you take a defeat. That's what really matters. It was a tough one for you to swallow, too. You've never had to take many lickings in your life. You've always been on top."

"Not lately, Dad. Not since I left home."

"Oh? No? Well, I imagine you've been through some thin times this summer. Just the same, you haven't had much experience in losing and, believe me, I was proud of you yesterday. I watched the way you handled yourself with those sports writers in the lockers afterwards—no alibis, no excuses. I was waiting for you to say something about strange clubs. You didn't. They had to drag it out of you.

Now one more thing, Bob. I do want to tell you how wrong I was back there the night we talked about your leaving, back in June. I said you'd never amount to anything as a golfer. Remember? Well . . . I was wrong. You can be one of the best if you stay with it and practice and work."

"You really think so, Dad, you think so after yesterday?"

"Forget yesterday, will you please? Yes, I do sincerely think so, and the man from the *New York Times* does too. He was talking with me while you were dressing last night. Know exactly what he said? Said you made him think of Hogan as a youngster."

"No! Honest? Gosh, that's terrific!"

Bob's head went back on the seat. Now that the strain of the trip was over, he felt far more tired than he had since the fire on the Donner Pass. For in a way he had been on his toes every minute; never could he relax; never did he know what the next day would bring, how he would get a ride, where he would sleep, what he would eat if he did eat. Anyway, it was over, finished, done. He was seated comfortably in a plane en route to Idlewild and home.

He had wanted to get off on his own, to earn his way across the country and back again. Well, he had done it; he hadn't quit, he had succeeded.

His eyes closed. He went back over the past weeks, thinking especially of some of the people he had met: of the bakery man who gave him his first ride in a grim moment; of the unknown farmer who saved him from quitting cold that day outside Iowa City; of the salesman who bought him a big dinner when he hadn't eaten a real meal for two days; of Hugh Gathwick, resourceful, cool, competent, who taught a native so much about the art of hitchhiking; of the big rancher who almost knocked him across the counter at Guide Rock, Nevada; of Scotty, the diesel specialist, who had served a term in jail and who had almost won a national golf title. Bob remembered the kind, warm Americans who had befriended him all the way across the country. And the cops who had not.

He thought of the great cities he had passed through. Again he saw the Continental Divide against the sky, those snow-capped peaks where the rivers on one side flowed south and east, and on the other, south and west. And all those other rivers he had crossed in crossing a nation: the Hudson, the Illinois, the brown Mississippi, the wide Missouri, the shallow Platte, the Colorado, the Muddy, the Green, the Sacramento, the San Joaquin. What a huge, wonderful country! How fortunate I've been to see it, to feel it, to know it . . . a little!

"Wake up, son! We're coming into Idlewild."

Bob's mother met them at the airport. Bob saw her as they came up the ramp, slim and pretty. Why, she's young-looking, just as Dad is, he thought. A guy is lucky to have parents like this, not fat ancients like some of the people who picked me up on the road between here and the Coast.

They piled into the car, all laughing and talking together, and they let him drive. Fortunately, his mother did not notice that he was without his precious clubs, so no mention of them was made. She was too busy telling him the news, what had happened at home, how glad she was to have him back at last, how the *Times* had such a fine write-up of the tournament.

"And, Robin, that was such a wonderful account of that forest fire you went through. We read it and reread it, and Dad took it to the office . . ."

"Oh, Mother!" He was not sure that he liked that, yet he did not dislike it, either. "By the way, Dad." He pulled a white Hotel Statler envelope from his pocket, for Dad always handed over money in an envelope. "By the way, here's that twenty."

"That what?"

"That twenty. You know, the twenty you gave me when I left. I promised to pay it back. Remember?"

There was a moment or two of silence. Then Dad did the right thing. "Thank you," he said seriously, and took the envelope, stuffing it into his side pocket.

They left the Hutchinson River Parkway and zoomed along the Merritt Highway. Connecticut—how many times I've thought about it. Why, I'm just as much a nut as the folks in California, he laughed to himself. I love this state the same way they love theirs.

Then they were turning off at the exit, going through the town and up West Side Avenue to the house. Exactly as he had left it. Fanny greeted him at the front door. She inspected him closely.

"My . . . how he has grown . . . he has grown . . . he's older, too, much older. 'Pears like it does him good to get away from us."

He took his bag upstairs to his room, his own room, not a hotel room or a cubbyhole in a Y., but his room with the three big windows facing the water, with Dad's blue Yale flag across one side wall.

Why, I even feel different about Yale, now I've been away and come back. Yale seems different here, where everybody takes it for granted, from the way it seems when you're alone on the prairie in the middle of nowhere. Yale, the place they called the rich man's school. I never let them get away with that, though!

It's sure good to be home, he thought, looking round, touching familiar objects: his books, the pictures of the track team hanging on the wall, his bed. He sat on it. How many times I've longed for this bed in the past months!

He took a shower and dressed in his usual summer costume, dark blue shorts and a clean white skivvy shirt. It was a hot September day and the Sound sparkled in the sunshine. Through the open win-

dows he saw sloops, yawls, and small boats just beyond the harbor entrance, their sails making big
balloons against the blue water. The yacht club was
out; a race was going on over toward Long Island,
and some of the boats were tacking into the wind.
Motorboats roared, came rushing into the harbor
entrance, slacked off, glided up and caught their
moorings. He had seen these things a million times.
Now they were fresh and new, yet familiar and homelike, too.

This is part of me, he thought. I wouldn't really
be happy far from this coast. A fine place, California;
Californians, you can't help liking them. But what
made me think I wanted to go to school out there?

He raced down, three steps at a time, out to the
porch and the lawn below. The screen door banged
with the customary sound. He recognized many of
the boats below like old friends: the Rands' big white
yacht tied at its pier up the river, the Masons' boat
with the faded pink sails, the Waterburys' blue yawl
—all at their accustomed moorings. Exactly as he
had left them, two and a half months before.

Across the water in Five Mile River, cars were
going up and down Sound View Avenue. The line
of red shipyards seemed as busy as ever. Like giant
bees in the late summer haze, the hum and buzz of
the electric saws came over to his ears.

The grass was thick and yielding to his feet. He
walked around the house, where a pile of long poles

leaned up in one corner. He hefted two or three and took one. Practice, that's what it takes to be any good. Pole vaulting, golf, hitchhiking, it's all the same. You've got to work if you want to be tops. Everything depends on the individual.

He tumbled down on the grass, tossing aside the pole, rolling over and over in delight. Then he turned on his back, flexing his legs and kicking them furiously into the air. He rolled over on his stomach and did half a dozen push-ups; he waited a minute and did half a dozen more. Next he rose and trotted up and down the familiar path, observing with surprise that it was now green and completely grown over. He sprinted hard at the bars, raced between the uprights, returned and repeated the process. Then, with care, he placed the bar at twelve feet. He used to start at eleven, but now he had been in the big time; he had competed with a Californian. Out there they start at twelve.

A speedboat snarled angrily out in the Sound. It seemed good to hear that accustomed noise again. Standing motionless, balanced on his toes, the pole at his side, he started slowly. Then, gathering speed, he went into his sprint. His body rose and arched against the sky. He straightened out, clearing the bar, and landed on all fours like a cat in the pit below.

"Robin! Oh, Robin! You're wanted on the telephone."

Without glancing, he knew his mother was calling from the kitchen window. Rising, he slapped the dirt from his shorts.

"Robin!" She called again.

"Bob, Mother! Please call me Bob."

"Oh. Oh, yes . . . Bob. It's Pamela Griswold. She wants to hear about your trip. She says would you care to go for a sail in their new boat? Please come, Robin . . . I mean Bob. She wants to talk to you."

"O.K., Mother. I'll be right there."